Fire In The Night
And Other Stories

The 2014 Writivism Anthology

Fire In The Night and Other Stories

THE 2014 WRITIVISM ANTHOLOGY

UK/International editions published by
Kushinda ISBN 978-0957142046
www.kushinda.com
African edition published by Boda Books
(A CACE imprint)

Edited by Sumayya Lee

Cover Design by Rukundo Joshua

CONTENTS

FOREWORD

It has been an honour to edit the 14 stories longlisted for the 2014 Writivism Short Story competition. Kudos to the *Centre for African Cultural Excellence* who have provided platforms for our stories - long may it fulfil its commitment to nurturing the Arts in Africa.

As a child, I believed that everyone loved stories. Period. It didn't matter where they were set, they simply needed to be captivating. Fast forward to the 21st century and the internet is crammed with discussions on *African* Literature. Should our stories be issue-based or idyllic characterisations that fit the PR image of the continent? The website *africaisacountry.com* presented a collection of African Books, pointing out that the sun rising, or setting spectacularly behind an acacia tree, has come to represent Africa. All the covers mirrored this image.

While the world may be comfortable with images that present Otherness in ways that are easy to understand, we must not allow this Otherness to penetrate our writing. Bookshops in Africa need to assimilate our work into the mainstream, so that this Otherness does not affect the reader's choice either. Ben Okri, in his recent BooksLive interview says, "Writings from Africans need to be perceived purely as writing and not prefixed with the continent."

I am with Okri on pushing forward and losing the prefix. Let us write what we will, giving voice to the poor *and* the privileged, the unbridled optimism *and* the depths of despair. The full range of human emotion and experience set against our vast and varied rural *and* urban terrain.

If a novel is a film, a Short Story is anything from a photograph to a YouTube clip. The essence of a Short Story has been described as a punch in the gut. This anthology more than satisfies the above criteria while exhibiting a diverse, multi-cultural Africa.

The stories open windows on lives we may not know, events we cannot understand - like Sseguja's *Walls and Borders*, a disturbing tale of a Rwandan refugee searching for her home. Or Ugbede's *Day After Tomorrow* and its grappling with the madness that is often associated with Africa. Sadly, all Africans are au fait with varying degrees of corruption, and Ngasa's *Devils* speaks boldly to us all.

There is dissonance in the form of Mwale's *Fire in the Night* and Bhamjee's *Lunatic*, both discomfiting but beautifully written stories. Coming of age and defying tradition are entertainingly tackled by Atemnkeng's *My Breasts*. I am ashamed that I was aware of foot-binding in China yet had no idea Breast-Ironing pubescent girls was practised in the Cameroon.

Kiguwa raises questions of identity in *The Wound of Shrinking* with aesthetic grace, a grace that colours Musalia's tale of magical realism *Kawesa* and Preen's sad but satisfying *The Gift*. Bamjee and Lawal approach idiosyncratic notions of Motherhood with aplomb in *Out of the Blue* and *Dr Lawanson*. Human relationships and bizarre families are reflected in Kasese's *Inside Outside* and Njoku's *Survived By*. Paquita's *Friday Night* is a zany portrayal of Born Free angst in Cape Town.

I invite you to be entertained, amused and disturbed - to celebrate common humanity while getting acquainted with Africa. Let our book covers make room for the Kolanut Tree *and* the mighty Baobab. And let our stories be perceived as stories. Let us not be the Other in *our* land.

Sumayya Lee
London, May 2014
Author: The Story of Maha / Maha, Ever After

SHORTLISTED STORIES

DEVILS
Wise Nzikie Ngasa

"This country is fucked up. What shit are they celebrating?" Mbatu nods towards the noisy bunch of students who have occupied every table in this open-air bar. They are singing and dancing as if someone just won a million dollars in the lottery. These are the boys and girls who say they have 'swag'. Girls in tight, revealing shorts, on heels as high as Caterpillars, lips glowing from all the lipstick shades in the world. Boys with trousers hanging below their bums, drinking straight from bottles and puffing cigarette smoke high into the air. They wear shiny 'bling' on their wrists, waists, ankles, noses, teeth, navels and tongues. They drink beer like water; our fathers taught us well.

Naked girls are shaking and pushing their plump behinds into the faces of excited boys at the far end of the bar.

"Boy," Mbatu cries. "What is there to celebrate, apart from naked girls?"

"Youth Day, Mbatu. Youth Day for God's sake!" Brenda shouts.

She has to shout. The blasting of music from gigantic speakers, the screaming of inebriated youth, of okadas skidding past - these have all come together to construct a clamour that is loud enough to win one of those stupid prizes on offer everywhere.

Youth Day indeed. We are celebrating our failures, the felonious gaffes of our fathers, the funeral of youth participation in nation building, our haunting frustrations. I pity the African youth, whom I believe in so much. We deserve better than cheap bottles of beer, high schools for universities, dusty roads, no water, no electricity, jobs that pay five hundred an hour. We do not deserve the lies and the insults. The insults!

We cannot afford to spend all our time complaining about the failures of the past. But we must! We must complain without fear. We must tell them that they failed both themselves and posterity. We must vehemently dispute the unending fib and slur, the intellectual fraudulence, the tributes paid to murderous mediocrity. We must ask them to bring back our money from Swiss bank accounts. But we must go further than grumbling. We must ...

3

I draw inspiration from my bottle.

Sitting around and fuming has never done any good to mankind. We have nine bottles on the table and I am beginning to feel uncomfortable. I signal to an idle waiter to clear up. The idiot ignores me and walks away dragging his feet on the floor. Brenda frowns and sighs.

"You're fired!" she shouts after him. "Did you see that? I'd have him fired if this were my business. Isn't that mean?"

Nobody replies.

"Shit." She sighs. "Shit." Brenda takes out a mirror and powder and begins to dab gently at her face.

Mbatu sneers. "Brenda, this is a bar. Can't we just drink and forget about how ugly you look? You get older each time you add another layer of that stupid dust to your face."

"Guys, let's move," I say quickly, to clear the air.

It is one o' clock in the morning when we hit the Rocket, an underground club shaped like one. We make our way down the first staircase. There are mirrors, and posters of boys with six packs and sparkly girls at the foot of each staircase. Three such staircases lead into the ground where the rocket emanates.

As we descend, the cold air from above begins to give way to new exhilarating warmth: to the din of sweet music, the smell of smoke and alcohol, to the breath of sweaty humans and pungent perfume. Rocket has a dance floor that cannot be larger than ten square-metres, held up by four pillars around which a lot of things are happening.

The pillars carry loud speakers, flashing lights and mirrors. One can barely see those on the dance floor; they have been misplaced in a mist that is blowing across the hall. As the gas drifts away, they slowly begin to appear, like agitated ghosts in a cloud of white smoke.

The waitresses in their black and white skin-tight tops and miniskirts follow us to our table with Jack Daniels, Baileys, ice, olives, and Coke. Mbatu takes out his wallet and pays nonchalantly. We pour ourselves drinks and toast to the day - to this one moment when we can forget about all those who have worked so hard to put this country in shambles. We just want to have fun. From the corner of my eye, I spot a girl dancing in a mirror and kids

4

kissing in the VIP. There is smoke and lust in the air and I am glad we came. We are here for the good life, for a share of the sweet raw pleasures that only badly lit places like this can offer. The lights are flashing, the music is loud, the DJ is singing the praises of some guy who has gotten all the girls in the neighbourhood pregnant and the girls love it!

Mbatu keeps saying this is cool, this is cool. He pops the collar of his shirt, he smiles. He licks his thick lips. He looks around arrogantly. Mbatu is lust and arrogance. He gets up and approaches the girl in the mirror. He starts dancing with her. He is whispering into her ears. He sure knows how to dance and talk big around the ladies.

Brenda rises to her feet and draws me up. We find a space on the dance floor and begin to dance. Makossa from the good old days is playing and we are killing it on the dance floor.

Body temperatures rising, girls screaming, kids dancing and frolicking to raw music. Jack in my blood. Everything is coming together in a bad way. This is cool. There is a thing in my head: a maddening buzz like a feather-light spirit that consumes you and makes you high. I feel hot, elated, and gutsy.

I cannot recall clearly, but it must have taken me a while to realize that something was wrong. I remember noticing the guys on the other end of the hall moving aside and the girl in the mirror and other girls screaming their lungs out. The music stopped. The bouncers ran into the club and the bright lights were turned on.

Mbatu was lying on the floor. Then I saw his tongue, hanging out of his mouth like a big wet snake. I ran to him. Blood poured generously out of invisible taps - he must have been stabbed many times. I tried to stop it and was soon soaking in a red river of his blood. I think the bouncers and I dragged him out of the club, up the staircases and into the car, which a crying Brenda had driven to the entrance.

I remember Brenda thumping the horn and accelerator in mad fury as we charged away from the parking lot. She whizzed through the exit drive of the Rocket, towards the motorbike in front of us until we almost knocked it down. The rider gave way in perilous haste, fuming and cursing in disbelief. Mbatu lay fully stretched out on the back seat with his head on my knees. He was bleeding profusely and I tucked the cloth frantically around his wounds.

"Mbatu, please stay with us," I pleaded.

His eyes rolled open for a while and he coughed a smile. It was a courageous smile meant to reassure us. Instead, I found the pain in my stomach solidifying. I felt all the emotions in my body coming together at a single point somewhere inside me and then dispersing throughout my body, slowly tearing me apart.

I looked out of the window but in the darkness and pain I barely noticed the dirty buildings and the mud walls flying past, the rubbish heap right at the centre of the road where street children with rashes all over their bodies and pigs wrestled for something to eat. The car swerved abruptly as Brenda struggled to dodge a lake that had appeared suddenly.

My throat itched. My heart was pumping as if I had just awoken from the most dreadful nightmare. I opened my mouth but nothing came out. The words dissolved before they could be spoken.

"Samba," Brenda said. "Everything will be fine. Okay?" I nodded.

"How is he now?"

"I think he is fine," I said hastily, wanting it to be so. It had to be so. I wanted to tell Brenda that I could feel Mbatu's spirit leaving us, but I feared that it would happen if I talked about it. I could see the determination burning in Brenda's eyes.

"Samba," Mbatu whispered weakly and smiled, but this time he did not open his eyes. His lips parted weakly, "Brenda, where is she?"

"Right here," Brenda said with a finger on the horn. It had not stopped blaring since we drove onto the highway.

"Just drive on sweetheart. Everything will be fine. How long before we get to the hospital?"

"We're almost there," I murmured.

We left the Commercial Avenue and sped towards the Hospital Roundabout. A police checkpoint suddenly came into view at the next street light.

"Devils!" Brenda screamed. "They set up road blocks even in the centre of the city? This is senseless. This is

6

insane."

A cop stepped onto the road, holding up his right hand. "Shit!" Brenda applied the brakes and the car squealed to a halt.

A blue police van was parked nearby with a number of police officers standing around. The cop, a bushy man with the stench of alcohol on his breath at three in the morning waved a flash light and put his chunky head through the car window. The urgency of the moment left me with no option but to develop an instant abhorrence for his existence.

"Vos papiers Madame," he said in French. Greed and corruption were written all over his thick face.

"Officer, we don't have time for this." Brenda spat out the words like hot potatoes. "My friend is dying and we need to take him to the hospital now. We have everything. You will see them on our way back."

"Really?" the black bulbous fool hissed as he stared through the window at the blood on my shirt. "Really?" he asked again with stonehearted indifference. His eyes glistened with immoral arrogance.

Brenda clutched at the wheel in a mad rage and I prayed that she would not do anything rash. One of the officers had pushed a barricade onto the road.

"Your papers, let me see them," he smiled, revealing nasty brown choppers. His dirty uniform hung over his pot belly like the flag of shame.

"Don't you see the blood?" Brenda yelled. "I said the man is dying!"

Mbatu shuddered.

"Your papers," the officer ordered calmly. Brenda searched around hoping to find them.

"Officer, I'm sorry," I sputtered. "I'm afraid we don't have them. Please. We need to get to the hospital."

"Great! Great!" the officer said, unable to conceal his delight. "You tell me that you have papers, you even go ahead to shout at a commissioned officer and now you don't have them anymore? You know what to do when you don't have papers, don't"I don't. Just do whatever you have to do and get out of the way, Mr. Officer," Brenda said with raw sarcasm.

"No, no. It's up to you young woman. You are old enough to know what is good for an officer. Aren't you?" he beamed wickedly.

I was boiling over. I was about to detonate. Bubbles of rage had accumulated, burning at the tissues in my throat. I was thirsty. I had seen it before, many times before. This time however, I did not see it coming. That a skunk, a five star numbskull - would stop us and ask for a bribe so openly while Mbatu's blood was pouring down my shirt – was ... God! This was blatant, uncensored greed. Greed that could drive even Mephistopheles mad.

I wanted to reach out for the officer's gun and put a bullet in his skull. I wanted to kill him. I had always believed nobody has the right to take another man's life, but at that moment all I wanted to do was slaughter him. I wanted to peel his skin and lay bare the arteries and veins in his neck.

And yet I realized that it was not the man I really wanted to destroy. It was the greed. The culture of corruption and the perennial disrespect for the law. Even at the expense of the life of a good man. But what is a vice without a man? How could I do away with a vice without destroying the man in whom it had been introduced and nurtured and allowed to prosper?

Brenda began to search frantically in the glove compartment. Mbatu coughed and cleared his throat.

"No one is going to give a bribe here,' he whispered painfully. 'Not today guys." His lips were twisted, his teeth prattled as he spoke. His face, however, was that of one who was at peace with himself.

I had heard that people do strange things when they are about to die and Mbatu's words could not have been stranger.

"Mbatu, you are dying ..." I reminded him. "So be it," he cut me off softly.

The numbness in my body gave way. I was taken captive by a new wave of desperation. Brenda had stopped talking. She was holding her head in her hands.

"Mbatu, I am sorry," she said slowly, reaching for something in her hip pocket, "but we can't let you die like this.""Brenda," Mbatu whispered the name with a note of authority. His face contorted in pain. It was like he was summoning the

8

spirits, gathering all that was left in him, all his strength and potency.

"Take my hand," he ordered. Brenda took his hand and caressed it lovingly.

His voice was fading; we had to lean close to catch the waves of his whispers. "Do not defy the wish of a dying man." He lay back and smiled kindly at us.

There was a long silence. An officer who had been standing close by came towards us.

"I think you should let them go," he said to his colleague. "This is blood money man," he said as he walked away.

The idiot contemplated for a moment before retreating unwillingly.

"Inspector Patrick," Brenda said, reading from the badge on the officer's shirt as we drove past. "You will hear from me if something happens to my friend, you rotten piece of shit!"

I was no longer a part of the world. Mbatu's utterances had lifted me past the skies. I was floating nowhere in a state of wondrous adoration and reverence for him.

"Devils!" Brenda screeched as she steered the jeep to the centre of the road and raced all the way to the hospital.

Mbatu had passed out by the time we got there though the bleeding had slowed down. The place was teeming with sick people but doctors and paramedics were visibly absent. A boy helped us carry Mbatu through a sea of miserable eyes to the emergency room. A nurse was leaving the room as we came in.

I ran after her. "My friend is dying, someone has to attend to him now," I said desperately.

She stopped in her tracks, looked me over and walked away without saying a word. I laughed, but it was not really a laugh. It could have been anything. I had become immune to shock. I ran back inside.

Mbatu had been placed on a bench. There was a woman with a rotten leg hanging painfully on crutches, and a kid who had lost both eyes in a fire, and six or seven people with unimaginable injuries lying on the bare floor. "I think we are losing him," I told Brenda. She nodded and kept on pacing up and down the room.

A long neck appeared at the door. She said a doctor was

on the way and disappeared again. Brenda ran out, calling after her, but she would not stop. She shot forward and in a moment of madness grabbed the nurse roughly from behind and pinned her to the wall by her neck. I held my breath and waited. Somebody ran up to them and pulled Brenda away. The nurse rubbed her neck and hurried away as if nothing had happened.

I went back inside and waited. Brenda came back, swearing at the Devils and we went over to Mbatu and sat on the edge of the bench where he lay. We sat there wondering how a single doctor could attend to the score of critically injured people in the room. I sat there thinking about all the taxes that we had faithfully paid to Caesar. I sat there cursing the people for their inability to hold the Devils to account. We sat there for fifteen minutes, and then thirty minutes, and the doctor who was on his way still did not arrive. We sat there losing hope, pretending that everything was going to be fine.

LUNATIC

Saaleha Bhamjee

Fear *has* a taste. It is this metallic tang that floods my mouth as I quicken my steps. My heart is a frantic tattoo, my mouth impossibly dry. I swallow. My tongue glues itself to the roof of my mouth. I squeeze Fatima's hand and feel her answering squeeze. My breaths slow. And then the moment is gone and I am drowning once more.

Where *is* he?

I scour the dirty Dadaville streets, willing Zaahid to appear.

Why does he *do* these things? Doesn't he know I need him? Is he really no better than his bastard father? The man who abandoned us when he learnt of my pregnancy.

I remember that day. How I twisted words, bent them, spread them. I even poked with them, hoping, hoping for something. He didn't want the child. It was there in the corded arms that framed his rigid form. Arms that had once cradled all my hopes. His lips, an ugly scratch on his face; jaw, flinty. Zaahid has those lips. Curved so rarely in a smile of late. A jaw as impervious as his father's.

"Say something! Tell me you love me! That you will take care of us ..."

My words just bounced off his armour of silence, fell at his feet. He stepped over them. Click. A door in my face, cutting off my soliloquy, banishing every hope. He stepped into the June air. I saw his breath rise in clouds before his face, saw it vanish. Saw him vanish.

My fear struggles to keep up with my mounting anger; palms slick. Rayhana's hand squirms inside my own and I loosen my grip. It is too late though. I've dragged them with me, deep into my despair. And still I race. Searching, not finding. Fatima stumbles, I slow down

What kind of son is he? The ingrate! After everything I've been through for him! After everything I've endured to keep a roof over his head and food in his stomach!

Sixteen years. SIXTEEN fucking years!

Shanawaaz at the Corner Cafe, where his gang, The Kajala Boys hang out, hasn't seen him. Neither has Ice Man (real name, Arshad), the leader of the Kajalas.

As the sun burns itself out, swallowed by a line of tin roofed houses, my gut clenches tighter. I don't notice the colours that stain the sky. Barely register that an entire bank of frothing cloud has a silver lining.

I can delay no longer. Anu will be home. Anu will be waiting. And Anu doesn't like waiting ...

Fear wins.

As I round the corner, I see him. A statue at the gate. And I know. I drag my feet as I approach. Both girls cling to my hands. I catch Fatima's gaze as she steals a look at my face. A fat tear wobbles on her lower lashes. I can almost taste its salt in my own fear. There is nowhere to run. I accept this. But I can delay, can't I? Just a little? For them?

He does not shout. Not today. He just takes my hand and pulls me into the house, locking the bewildered girls outside. There is no smell of liquor on his breath. And somehow, I know that today it will be worse.

He pushes me into our bedroom. Shuts the door. A gunshot! I flinch.

"Strip." His voice like broken glass.

I stand, looking stupidly at his quivering face.

"Strip, you fucking hoer meit!" He grabs my dress, pulls me towards his chest and rips it.

He shoves me onto the bed. I watch his hand slide over the buckle of his belt. His movements, deft.

I hunker, arms shielding my face, eyes squeezed shut, waiting to hear the familiar whistle of the belt. I'm completely oblivious to my nakedness. My blood pounding against my eardrums drowns out the sound of my girls, pummelling the front door with their fists.

His weight bearing down on me catches me by surprise. And then he is on top of me. Thrusting. Prying my legs open. I lie very still. Do not struggle. This is *not* happening. Surely that woman, so small, so fragile, lying spread eagled on a floral bedspread, she is not me. Surely that man, he is not Anu. He could never be my Anu.

With each thrust, I begin to feel something inside of me breaking. Crumbling. Leaving a gaping abyss that swallows all my fears. All my anxieties. Everything ...

By the time he shudders, lies still for a moment before rolling off me, I know ... It has to be done.

He stands up, steps into his pants without even wiping.

"Just remember, bitch. I own you. Don't go looking for that half-caste bastard of yours when I am waiting here to be fed a decent meal. I work damn hard to look after all of you."

The words do not sting.

I lie there, naked, legs scissored, until I hear him settle in the lounge, switch on the TV. Then I stand up, wrapping the bedspread around myself. It is stained. I'll have to wash it. I go to the bathroom. I do not let the girls in. Their whimpering is abstract. Like death. I cannot own it. Not today. Not like I've owned all their tears since the day each of them was lowered into my arms, squalling, wailing purpose into my life.

I shower, dress, rinse out the stain on the bedspread in the basin, straighten the bedroom and then open up for them. Rayhana has fallen asleep, her head cradled on Fatima's bony lap. I go to wake her. She is reluctant to wake. I notice how the tears that have dried on her face leave white streaks that age her. When she finally staggers to her feet, her eyes are sad. Scared. My words evaporate.

Fatima's eyes speak questions. I cannot meet them.

That night I lie in bed, eyes shut, replaying my annihilation on a loop. I feel his weight settle beside me on the bed. His leg brushes against my own. I recoil, but do not stir. He strokes my brow. Bile rises to my throat. I do not blink when I feel his scalding tears fall onto my cheeks. Do not answer when I hear him whisper.

"Why? Why must you make me so angry? Why do you keep on doing these things? Like a stupid hoer meit! Don't you know I love you?"

***

13

His snores bounce off the white walls of our bedroom. I study the planes of his face and listen so long that the sound seems to vibrate within me.

The years fold in on themselves. He is whole, once again, wooing me, a single mother with a love child borne of little love. A beautiful man, bearing flowers, chocolates. Crooning.

"Hello, is it me you're looking for?"

I was so young, so stupid. Collecting his promises like prayers. The opiate that dulled the pain from my father's slaps. Weakened the poison in his insults. With My Anu, I wasn't just 'a stupid hoer meit, fucking every guy with a few rands in his wallet.' I was more than just the 'mother of a bastard that even his own father didn't want.' I wasn't a 'slut just like your mother.'

He made me feel beautiful. With him, I *was* beautiful.

No musallee bowing down five times a day in the masjid believes in Allah more than I believed in Anu.

The first time he slapped me, I saw it as a test of my faith. Doesn't Allah always test the slaves He loves? I would pass. My faith would not waver. My god brought me flowers, even wept when he apologised. That night we made such sweet love. It was the night we made Fatima.

All through my pregnancy, he was attentive. Truly a love god. Zaahid would follow him on dimpled four-year-old legs, everywhere he went, as worshipful as I was. How did I get so lucky?

Faith is so easy when the goings are good.

I read his face again. His jowls quiver each time he exhales. In repose, his mouth is not so hateful. It does not spew vitriol. It is soft. Where once, the memory of his mouth moving against my flesh would cause a stirring in my loins, now it fills me with self-loathing.

His neck is no longer as firm; the skin sags, obliterating those once irresistible hollows at the base of his neck. *I want to crawl into those hollows. Curl up and sleep. Feel your pulse even in my dreams.* His hair is finer and his receding hairline lends a near comical aspect to his face. How come I'd never noticed before today, what a weak jaw he has? In the wrong light, he's almost ugly.

I stare long, wondering if perhaps today I'll feel

14

something. He stirs.

Nothing.

My detachment doesn't surprise me anymore. It has been a protracted death, its final breath, not some whimpering sigh, like a candle being snuffed out, but a blood curdling wail. A sound dredged up from the darkest corner of my soul the day my Zaahid left.

My boy. Gone. Just like that. Not even a word for his mother. No hugs for his sisters. Just a cold bed, waiting for me one morning when I went to wake him for work. His cupboard, almost intact. I sank onto his bed and howled.

I should have walked out all those years ago. After my first broken rib. Anu's boots had been so hard that night. Zaahid's fear, so loud.

The neighbours watched from behind their thick curtains. Lights switched off. I could feel their eyes on us. So many watchful eyes, all pouring shame onto my wounds, making them sting even more. Boring into me. Greedy eyes that swooped on every inch of my being that became exposed under Anu's fists.

Zaahid, 10 at the time, running door to door.

"Uncle, uncle, please! Please, please uncle, help my mummy!" Even through the haze of my pain, I could hear his hysteria. I wanted him to stop. Just stop!

"Aunty Faye. Please Aunty Faye. You're mummy's friend. Please, someone help her. He'll kill her!" His sobbing pierced the silence, clear as shame.

Not a single door opened.

Anu had my head pressed into the bonnet of his car. I remember patterns. Red blooms of blood, flowering everywhere I touched. He smashed my head into the bonnet, again and again, tearing at my hair.

The last thing I saw before I passed out was my daughters, pooled on the pavement. Zaahid, his arms wrapped around them, hiding my disgrace from them, holding them together, so they wouldn't splinter like Anu's car window had when he banged my head into it. Falling to the ground in a shower of sparkly shards that caught the light so prettily, I almost smiled.

I woke to find myself inside an ambulance, the street

15

awash with the eerie blue and red lights that herald calamity.

"You should leave him, Miss."

What did she know? All of twenty, a paramedic, earning her own money, no children to fend for?

Even now, when I think back to the look the police officers gave me when I said I didn't want to give a statement since I wouldn't be pressing charges, I burn. Was I really worth so little?

Faye suggested the local Imam. He could annul the marriage. My skin still crawls when I remember how his too-soft-for-a-man hand had travelled up my dress, as he bent to 'study' my bruises.

Perhaps it is too late for Zaahid and I. But the girls, I can still save my girls.

* * *

They come out of their houses and stand on the grimy sidewalk, gawping. A grown man, ranting and raving, throwing dishes about, threatening to kill his wife and children; threatening to kill himself.

Yissus! He's behaving like a blerry child. No brains! This is what they whisper to one another when he goes back into the house. Nobody dares talk while he is on the stoep! No telling what the lunatic will do!

Half an hour passes. She steps out of the house, lugging a heavy bag. Her girls hold hands. They look terrified. He follows her. Tries to touch her. She turns to face him. Glares. He shrinks. They smile.

Did you see? Yoh! I never thought she'd ever do it! Sommer like that, nogal!

He looks ready to explode. Stands in the middle of the road, watching her until she turns the corner.

"Aarrrgghhh!"

They scurry back into their houses.

Ten minutes pass. His house is silent. They drift out again, converge like litter on the pavement.

It is then that it starts raining. Pots and pans. Plates and glasses. Bang. Smash. Crunch.

Ag, he's just looking for attention! Stupid! Look at that

vase that he just broke — Yissus! And it was cut glass too — No man, maybe he's just depresse — Hmph! Please, that's just rubbish! Since when Muslims get depressed, huh? It's his Iman. It's weak! I'm telling you! You know he drinks? — Hachoo? — Ya, my son told me.

No one bothers to ask her how her son knows. Oh no, now is not the time. Later, perhaps, they'll consider the riddle and reach their own conclusions.

Haai, maybe it's a Jinn. Ja, a jinn! You know my uncle Gulam?

Heads bob. There is no story so good as a Jinn story.

A Jinn got him. Yoh, he was so strong when the Jinn started with him, it took five of us to hold him down! And he could chow! One chicken was nothing for him.

More sage nodding.

Ja, a Jinn! It has to be. He has that wild look about him. His eyes look all black too. Of course no one attributes that to the darkness of the street.

You know, maybe I must tell his wife to take him to Moulana Adam. That Moulana is really good. Fatima's daughter had a Jinn. She used to scream, Maghrib time, every day. — Ja? — Ja, hachoo! The Moulana showed them when he cut the lemon on her, it had meat inside! So he said it was a Jinn that was troubling her. Eish! You should see her tear her clothes when he started burning the Ta'weez! Yoh! And how she screamed! Like one junglee! — Haai? Eish, they need to burn a few ta'weezes for this one here. — Eish, check, he's throwing her pots out of the house! — Duck! Here comes a thali!

They duck as a tray flies over their heads and lands with a clang on the warm tarmac.

He disappears into the house, comes out moments later, a gun in his hands. He points it first at them. They scatter; regroup in front of another house two doors up, craning their necks to see.

Whispers ripple through the crowd.

Eish! I think this guy's lost it man! —He sounds like he's crying, ne? — Yoh, he's mad! Now he wants his wife and daughters back! — You think he'll do it? — Eish! I don't know. — Must we phone her? — Nah, he's just acting. Guys that really want to kill

17

themselves don't stand in the street and make a show of it. You just do it! — If you ask me, I think it'll be better if he just did it. Will save that stupid woman a lot of trouble. 'Cos she don't have the guts to leave him. So many years! He takes her like a punching bag. — Haai, don't say that! —Check! Check! He's got it by his head jong! — Ag, you talking rubbish! I bet it's empty!

The blast rattles the windows, echoes. Blood splatters the wall.

WHAT THE FUCK! Quick! Come inside! The cops will come just now.

And they do.

OUT OF THE BLUE
Saaleha I Bamjee

It was always the most complete kind of feeling. Her head underwater, deaf to everything above the surface. Her ears opened to her own heartbeat and the residual of another from years ago, thrumming above the womb she nested in. She sucked water in and out of her mouth. It was her childish triumph, to breathe like this; absorbing oxygen through the mouth-lining, the cells pulsing with osmosis.

"You're not a fish Mariam," her mother had said. "You need gills to breathe underwater. You don't have any my girl. Don't be silly now or else you'll drown. Lift your head out of the water and breathe, like a normal person."

"But I'm not like a normal person, Mother," Mariam wanted to say but soon the water around her would turn to ink, her chest would fill with iron and she had to leave its hold to take the air in human fashion.

Mother was gone some ten years now, but in the water is where Mariam found her again, the rhythm of her cardiac cycle stronger along with the children Mariam lost and never had. Always there, in the depths, they swam on, together.

*

"I just can't be that transcendent," Mariam said, looking at her husband and back at the doctor. "I won't. If they're not my eggs, they're not my children. They'll start with David's seed and I'll carry them but all I'll really be is an incubator. I want my own children. My own."

Mariam's words stayed suspended in the consulting room. The doctor looked at the reports before him, shuffling them in exaggeration to slacken the tension between Mariam and David. He said he was sorry but there really wasn't anything else they could do. The last resort was for her to accept donor eggs. All possibilities had been exhausted.

Mariam wanted to scrunch up the word and aim it at his face. What did he know about exhaustion? He was just one specialist out of the ten they'd seen. It was her insides that had been constantly scraped for cells to be sent off for testing. She was the one who had to swallow and hold down fertility cocktails, never knowing what heinous side-effect would be present in the morning. Examination, re-examination, scan, rescan until all she saw when she looked in the mirror was a woman who carried below her belly, a planet that was incapable of sustaining life.

During the drive home from the doctor's rooms, Mariam waited for David to say something to her. Instead, he tuned the radio to a talk station where the presenters discussed the best time of year to plant amaryllis.

The anger piled onto her lap like unwieldy boxes, obscuring her vision. She was angry about everything; the incompetent doctors, her dead mother, David and his viable sperm, her own failure to carry a foetus to term, her eggs that had just been found defective, her biological imperative null and void.

David spoke when he pulled the car into their driveway. "I wish you would consider the procedure Mariam. The results are so promising." David, the pragmatist, always looking out for the best solution.

Mariam turned towards him and punched into his shoulder. "No. No. No. You're such a bloody man. Don't you understand? For once, think about how I feel."

David's eyes turned to smudged glass.

"That's all I've ever done, Mariam. I've tried so hard to be sensitive to what you're going through. But you just keep pushing me away. I want children Mariam and I want you. I don't want to have to make a choice."

The numbness set in just below her ribcage and spiked towards her heart.

"I can't have this conversation with you right now. I'm going for a swim," she said.

"That's your problem, you'd rather jump into the bloody water than have a serious discussion about our future together." Mariam didn't hear him, she was already out the door.

*When Mariam turned 32, her mother called to wish her a happy birthday and to tell Mariam that she had stage four liver cancer. "It's a waiting game now. I'm not taking the chemotherapy. I really don't want to prolong the discomfort. Please, don't make a fuss." Her mother may as well have been telling her that she'd lost her wallet and had to cancel all her credit cards.

"I did think I'd live to see my grandchildren but things don't always work out the way we want."

The family buried her four months later. At the tombstone unveiling, Mariam was the last to leave the graveside. Her eyes locked on to the epitaph 'Janet Reinhart 1952- 2010 She Loved Her Children'.

Her mother was not affectionate in the conventional sense. There were hugs and kisses on birthdays and when she and her brother brought home gold stars and trophies from school. In the Reinhart house, one was never pulled into a sloppy, squashy embrace without the reaching of a milestone as stimulus.

Mariam only felt close to her mother when they were in the water together. It was Janet who taught her how to swim, how to trust her own body in the water, to respect the depths and quell the treachery of panic by relaxing the muscles and to float off without a fight.

*

The silence in the house stretched thick over weeks and days until David said he was going away. To clear his head and the stuffiness in his heart. He'd be gone for a few days, enough space for them both to untangle their thoughts and for Mariam to decide how she wanted to proceed.

She drove him to the airport, feeling nothing but gaps and a canyon caught between their hugging arms. David's eyelids dammed the water as they kissed and Mariam turned her back to him all the way to an empty house.

In the days after David left, her routine pivoted around her swimming. If it wasn't for her interior design business and the clients she'd committed to, Mariam would have spent all her time in the water; pruning and ruminating. It was during her morning swim. She'd just taken one of her human breaths, her head just above the water, the sun slanting off of her shoulder blades, that she saw the boy in the street staring straight at her. The garden service left the gate open, providing an unguarded view into her backyard. She slapped back into the pool and out again. He was still there, watching her swim, transfixed.

He had the thrown-together appearance of someone who was used to taking whatever he'd been given.

Mariam rolled in the water, flipped onto her back. She floated for minutes, her mouth the only part of her above water. Another twist and she was back on her belly, her eyes turned towards the street. The child was gone. He was most likely a street urchin, a word her mother would have used. Mariam always liked the term twilight children, as if there was something a little whimsical and romantic about these vagabond spirits, belying the hardships of a day-to-day existence. Mariam's mood deflated and she emerged heavy from the pool to close the gate. It was getting cold and the water gave her nothing.

It was an uneasy night. Mariam tangled in the bedsheets, caught between too-hot and too-cold. She fell in and out of dreams that made villains of her mother and David. They wanted to strap her down to a bare metal table, spread her legs in the way witches used to be tortured and push pulsing free range chicken eggs up into her uterus. She kicked at them and ran but it was as if her legs had to struggle through set gelatine. Slow-motion horror. She choked awake. A light blinked from the night stand. A voice message from David on her phone. Mariam, this is really hard but I know we can make this work. I've been thinking about how you feel and it was insensitive of me to demand you just accept the alternative. I want to have children with you Mariam. I know you'll be a good mother. But if you can't go through what the doctor suggested, I respect that. I am willing to sacrifice everything for you. I love you.

Mariam heard David's voice break open just before he ended the call. A deep emptiness hollowed her. She went to the water.

The pool motor breathed heavy in the dark. Mariam switched on the backyard lights and walked towards the deep end. She preferred diving straight into bodies of water. The shock of the temperature, the rush of blood to the pores, the depth untested; it was how she wanted to live life. Being forewarned is to be disappointed. In this way she never had any expectations, except when it came to children. Who ever thinks they will never have their own children?

Tonight, the blue of the pool disturbed her. It was not complete. It held shadows that were not familiar. A lumpen black floated across. Not the silhouette of the Kreepy Krauly but something with a head and legs.

Mariam dived in. The chill of the water hit her like a wall. For the first time since learning how to swim at her mother's side, she lost breath and spluttered with frothing panic. She pushed her head back, allowed the water to hold her and sucked in air from just above the water line. Composed and calmer, her body spiralled towards the floating mass. It was a child.

Treading, she cradled the body as she pushed it towards the steps at the shallow end. The water pulled at her with the persistence of oil. Each movement heavier than the next, Mariam struggled against the viscous blue. Release me. Please. The water pulled and snapped back. Mariam tumbled onto the grassy border, still holding on to the child. The light revealed a young boy.

She lay him on his back and pumped his birdlike chest, wincing at the soft snap of rib just under her palm. She looked to the purple of his face and bent to meet it. He was too cold. His lips had swelled into the pout of a napping infant. All the innocence of the world cupped in those buds.

It was then that she noticed the pile of clothes at her side. It was the boy she'd seen in the morning. The twilight child. She remembered the orange t-shirt promoting an electrical supply company. The kind of thing that falls to the back of a cupboard, to be discovered during a spring-clean and discarded. It was the slogan that stuck on her mind; We Will Switch You On. Silly thing for a child to wear unless that's all he had. The cloth was marked with scorch marks, the hems unravelled. But for muddiness of the lawn, it was clean. There were shoes too, split soles and missing laces.

Mariam picked the boy up. Her arms moulded to his form. She felt no weight, but something warm beneath her sternum. She carried him into the house, a treasure chest from the depths, triumphant.

Fluffy towels would do for swaddling cloths. In the light of her bedroom, she studied him. He was a slender child, straight from shoulder to ankle. Like a line, simply overlooked and easily crossed. His skin bore the purple sheen from the water. His spooned against him. She laid her hand on his chest to seek out a telling beat but it was as if she pressed over hollowed wood. She held her ear to his mouth and heard only the void of a silent sea.

It occurred to her that sleeping beside a child that had just drowned in her swimming pool was rather macabre. But there was nothing ghoulish about the gift laid out next to her. Had he not been delivered unto her? Did she not bear him out of the depths? Was it not a labour that brought him out into the air?

She remembered the first baby she'd lost. She was too far gone in her pregnancy and had to push him out into a world he was already dead to. She remembered his pinched face and choked colouring. He didn't look like her or David, but something that had to have belonged to someone else, a cuckoo bird planted in her uterus while she slept. And after that, two more miscarriages. More imposters. Changelings to bury and mourn. She did not want another alien put inside her. But this child, he was hers. They'd been held by the same pulsing amniotic fluid, emerged from one womb, her brother-child. Not even a part of David, just hers and the deep.

She wondered about him before he came to her. The other life before this rebirth in her backyard. She imagined a long-suffering, hard-scrounging, desperate yearning for a home. He'd seen her in the pool and wanted to know his mother and now he was here and she would give him everything. She looked at his face again. The lips had parted further, revealing the gaps between his teeth in the kind of revealing perfection captured by a spontaneous photograph.

How long before her room would fill with the sweet decay of flowers. How long before she'd have to give him up? No, not just yet. She switched off the bedroom light and slept through the night.

The morning came upon her in a single act. She woke to startling brightness, her arm still across the dead child in her bed. A greyness had sunk into his pores. His face slacked. His skin had lost its yield. Mariam passed her hand over his forehead and tasted the hot salt from her eyes slide into her mouth. The phone on the bedside table beeped. A message from David. My Darling. I'm coming home today. I've had enough time to think. We'll talk soon. Properly. I promise. I love you.

The thought of David coming home filled her with a strange alchemy of hope and unsteadiness. In the last few days it was as if he was always just on the periphery of her experiences. A bystander, a sperm donor, a holder of her hand, a shoulder she crushed into during the hush of a velvet night. And now her wretchedness rose up in her throat. David deserved so much more, and she would be the one to give it to him.

She had to return her child to the water. Not to hide her strange night from David but to set her world right. This child of her heart, this child without a name, he was not really hers to keep.

The backyard was guiltless. The sun brushed silver against the pool's blue. The lawn looked lush; a paradise for ants. The garden service would be in the next day to trim the tips of the grass. They always took off a little too much. She liked it better when it was a bit overgrown. The pile high and tender, hiding her bare feet as she absorbed the cool green through her soles.

Today the child was heavier in her arms, his stiff limbs awkwardly angled. It was time.

She placed him on the grass closest to the edge of the pool. She dipped her hand into the water and drew a star on both his cheeks. They couldn't be gold ones but he would still leave being celebrated in some small way. Perhaps his real mother mourned him somewhere else, but here in Mariam's arms he was lucky to know of another love.

Her tears splashed across his receding lips and she leaned in to kiss him. Despite the rigidity of the boy's arms, she was able to pull off David's t-shirt with the grace of a magician. He was ready to be returned. And she slipped him back into the water.

She wanted to follow him. Listen again for the heartbeat, float on her belly like a pond lily, look for the face of her child. The pool was as receptive as ever but she pulled back.

There would be other children for her, ones who didn't need the water.

Mariam turned her face upward towards the sky; a warm blue expanse, depth-less and waiting.

SURVIVED BY

Kelechi Njoku

Mama wanted the hospital visits to stop, so she grumbled about this for days. At first, it seemed nobody in the family was listening to her. Then her youngest son Nwachi died. She grumbled louder. The hospital-going had to stop, she moaned, it had to stop. One morning, after breakfast, she slapped the hand of the person who came to administer her medications. The pills clattered to the floor and rolled in several directions. The person cursed and stormed out. In a minute, exasperated voices besieged Mama in the sitting room where she sat in an armchair, with a walking stick lying across her feet.

"You are acting like a child again, Mama!"

"Why do you want to stop going to the hospital anyway, eh?"

"Mama, you have to take your drugs, biko."

Mama did not bother working out who and who were speaking to her. It was pointless, her sight was a permanent blur. "Leave me alone!" she lisped at the voices. (Four of her front teeth were missing.) "Leave me alone, all of you. Get out of here."

A grey-haired man sat in the armchair beside her. His sagged chin rested on the crook of the walking stick clasped in his hands. He was Timothy, her son. He asked Mama – everybody – to calm down.

It was the week preceding Nwachi's funeral.

Nwachi had died last month. The funeral would have taken place the same month he died (February) but, as Mama had been told, Nwachi's oldest son Arinze – she believed that was his name – had been away in South Africa for important training that concerned journalists. Arinze – eh, that was his name – had returned two weeks ago, and the funeral preparations had only begun then.

"Leave me alone!" she said again, sensing people still around her. She hunched forward and pressed her palms to the arms of her chair. Her body quivered with the effort.

"Go and help Mama up," two voices cho014sed, all exasperation forgotten, and in a second, someone's hand came

26

to take hers and close it around the crook of the walking stick. The hands were smooth, their owner a young boy, Mama was sure from the breaking voice – "Where are you going?"

She offered the boy her hand. He pulled her gently to her feet. Her wrapper slid off her waist to the floor, exposing her thin legs up to the thighs and diapers bulging around her bottom. The boy quickly grabbed the wrapper and threw it around her waist. She slowly retied it.

"The bathroom," she said to the boy.

"Please give way, let a human being pass," she snapped as she and the boy shuffled through the small crowd of bodies towards the bathroom.

At the bathroom the boy made to open the door, but she asked him to knock first. He did. No reply. Nobody said to hold on let them finish. Mama sighed. This was normal. She shared this ground floor bathroom with three persons: Timothy, whose waist and knees were so painful he could no longer manage the stairs; his wife Malubia, who had retired from the civil service three years ago; and the help Doris, whose room, down the hall, was between Mama's and Timothy and Malubia's. The rest of the family, when they visited at Christmas, had different bathrooms and bedrooms they used upstairs. Malubia and Doris left early this morning for the market, and Mama had just been with Timothy in the sitting room; nobody could have been using the ground floor bathroom now. The entire arrangement, though made for her convenience, managed to feel like segregation.

* * *

The boy was waiting at the door when she came out of the bathroom. He slipped his hand around her waist and they shuffled back to the sitting room. It was deserted when they got there, except for Timothy still in his seat. The exasperated voices had gone. Upstairs, maybe. Mama stopped, as if to rest. She had never been upstairs since her children and older grandchildren contributed money to build this house – ten bedrooms, she had learned – a couple of years ago. She was already sick then. In fact, the year the house was completed, her arthritis had been so bad she could only move around in a wheelchair. The frequentness of the hospital visits had doubled, too. Every other week she would complain of a blinding ache behind her eyes, or how her meals sat heavy in her stomach without digesting.

Malubia would then ask her when she first started to notice this pain, this stomach trouble, and Mama would wonder what that had to do with anything, if answering the question would solve the problem. But she did not voice this snide remark – like she would have done many years ago, when Malubia had been a younger woman in her twenties, newly married to Timothy. Timothy had said it was the usual mother- and daughter-in-law friction, but Mama had ruled differently: Her son's wife just didn't know when to shelve her opinions. If her problem was not that all the knives in Mama's kitchen were blunter than wood, it was that ugu was supposed to be shredded with the fingers, not sliced with a knife, "to preserve the nutrients".

"We will go to the hospital tomorrow," Malubia said after Mama told her when the discomfort had begun. And the next morning, she would tie a scarf over her browning-and-greying hair and drive her husband's mother to the hospital; and Dr Ebuka would ask the same questions he had asked on several previous visits, and peer into Mama's eyes, and update her prescription – a frown zigzagging his eyebrows. It was around that time she was also diagnosed with urinary incontinence. Sometimes Timothy joined them to the hospital with complaints of his own – mostly about his knees – and Mama wondered at the madness of it all. How did her destiny bring her *here*?

Nwachi's death had jarred her. Worse than when her husband Paulinus was crushed in his car by a brake-failed trailor. (Paulinus whose expression used to blink between pride and gloom when he narrated how he shook the Princess Alexandra's gloved hand in 1960 while wondering if Independence hadn't come too soon.) But it had been different then, when Paulinus had died; Mama knew three or four other widows within their social circle. Today though, she could swear that every adult she had known at the time she married Paulinus – June 22, 1935, she couldn't forget the date – was dead.

The night she learned of Nwachi's death, Mama had lain in her bed, staring up at the ceiling, a rosary entangled in her fingers. Who would bury her when *she* died?

"Won't you sit down?" Timothy asked, steering her attention back to the sitting room.

The boy helped her back into her chair, and left the room. Soon, she heard his feet slapping up the stairs. "Do you want to say something I will not like?" she said. She straightened the edges of her wrapper with her gnarled hands.

Timothy grunted. His thick eyebrows shielded his sunken eyes. She could not have deciphered his thoughts by looking into his eyes even if she had been able to see them clearly. It had been like this ever since he was a little boy; she used to have to squat to look up into those eyes, to know if something was bothering him, or if he had misbehaved.

"I understand how you feel," Timothy said, "and I think the rest of the family does too. Old age is a burden to both the old and the young. It is as if we are dragging our children's lives back with our many problems."

Mama snorted. "You talk as if you are old."

"Am I not?"

"No. Wasn't it only yesterday I was still wiping shit off your bottom? You are not really old."

"I have arthritis and seven grandchildren, Mama."

"My child, you are only unfortunate. You may never be lucky like me. You should look after yourself properly," she said, mother to a son that still had much to learn about life. She shook her head, and fell silent.

* * *

Later that evening Mama joined the rest of the family in the dining room for dinner, and, when she was done, Doris put a small mound of pills into her palm, refilled her water glass, and placed the pills back in the small cupboard.

Mama swallowed the medicines without fuss. She set her empty glass down, and gripped the edge of the table, drawing on its solid strength for support.

A chair – or was that two chairs? – scraped back. Someone placed a hand on her back and put her walking stick in her right hand.

29

"Take Mama to bed," someone said needlessly.

The person who had just given Mama the walking stick raised Mama's left arm and hung it around their shoulders. The shoulders were small and sloped. A young girl. Teenage. Would this one be a grandchild or the child of a grandchild? Mama could not be certain. There were so many of her relatives who had arrived home for Nwachi's funeral. Some, she remembered their names and that they were this person's child or married to that other person who was her child or grandchild; others, she was not quite sure when they joined the family, if they belonged in the family. These details were small worries nowadays.

"Goodnight," she said to them.

"Goodnight, Mama," they said back, their chorus tangled with the clink of cutlery.

In Mama's bedroom the girl helped her change into fresh diapers and a peach nightgown; she sat on the bed, offering each weak hand to a sleeve as instructed. She lay down. The girl gathered her legs into the bed and covered them with a blanket. Mama thanked her.

"Who gave birth to you?" she said. "Patrick Ilo-Amadi is my father," the girl said.

Mama groped in her memory, searching for who Patrick Ilo-Amadi was. He wasn't any of her four children, three of whom were dead. No. The name rang familiar though. "Which of my children gave birth to your father, or is it your mother now?"

The girl paused for some seconds – probably trying to knit the threads of the family web in her head – and Mama concluded she might not know. She was very young after all. She would have known her grandparent by *Mama* or *Papa* if she'd met them at all.

"My father's mother was younger than Mpa Timothy," the girl said slowly.

Mama clasped her hands on her chest with an "Ah" of recognition. Her children: Caroline, Timothy, Ure, Nwachi. Born in that order. Ure was this girl's grandmother. She had died before any of her own children were married.

"You know what I remember the most about your grandmother?" she said to the girl. There was a smile in her voice.

"No, Mama."

"Trees. My daughter Ure loved to climb trees, like a boy. She was very healthy the day she died. She came back from school – she was a teacher like me in those days – ate lunch, went to the bathroom to urinate and had a heart attack. They found her on the toilet seat, like she had merely fallen asleep there."

The girl said nothing.

"What is your name, my child?"

"Jenny."

"Jenny. You will marry a good man. Will you not like that?"

"I will, Mama."

Mama grinned, showing the dark vacuum in her dentition. She wished she was not this tired all the time, this sick, weak, old. She would have gathered the young children of her family together and told them stories of the tortoise's craftiness, of extinct festivals and watered-down ones, of the days when children had to trek to the stream to fetch water before going to school.

"Is that pillow fine?" Jenny asked.

"Eh," she nodded. She pointed to the foot of the bed where there was a stool. "My rosary is there, give it to me."

Jenny found the rosary and brought it to her. "Goodnight, Mama." She snapped off the light on her way out, leaving Mama to think of darkness as emptiness and inexistence; and that, trapped in it, one felt alone in the sense of the only entity in existence; and that the spirit of God must have felt this way too in the beginning: alone and restless in the watery darkness. No wonder it had created – for company.

Mama remembered this feeling of aloneness from when she repeated Form 3. A long time ago now, around the time of the Aba Riots. That year, it wasn't her father's cane or the taunts of his other wives – and their children who didn't go to school – that had made her cry. No. It had been sitting in a classroom with pupils who used to be a class below her. It was looking around at their faces, while the teacher wrote on the blackboard, with the cruel realisation that her peers had gone ahead of her.

* * *

31

She rolled the rosary between her fingers. They felt warm because she had been clutching them a long time, and reassuring because she had known them forever. She prayed for her death long overdue.

Someone knocked on the door, entered and switched on the light, making her aware of other things in the room besides herself. She peered at the door.

"It's me," Timothy's blurry figure said.

He carried something that looked like a slim book. The manner in which he held it, thrust away from his body, stirred her interest.

"The funeral programme for next week," he explained. "The printer delivered them just now."

She took her gaze off him and faced the ceiling, her curiosity satisfied and lost. Why was he telling her?

"I came to show you something, Mama..." He leaned his walking stick against the bed, opened the programme to a page he must have marked earlier, and faced the page towards her, three feet between them.

Mama started to muster her strength to snap at him – how did he expect her to see that from where she was! What was wrong with this *child's* head? But Timothy went on talking. On this page she was looking at, he said, was listed everybody Nwachi was survived by: his widow Salome, five children, eight grandchildren, many nephews and nieces and cousins, Timothy himself (as brother), an uncle ... A total of fifty-three persons left to mourn him, Timothy said, and closed the page.

"Nwachi was the youngest of your children," he said, "yet he has so many of us surviving him."

Mama's chest heaved.

"It's not good for you to ... To harm yourself just because you think nobody will bury you when you ... "

"May thunder strike you dumb!" Mama hissed from somewhere deep in her stomach. Her slackened cheeks trembled under her rage. She clenched her fists, pressed her arms to the mattress to pull herself to a sitting position.

She failed and gave up. She asked Timothy if he did not know that the worst curse was to go grey with her own children, to bury them instead of them burying her. "Get out of this room and take your stupid talk with you, thunder strike you!"

And tomorrow – she resolved quietly as Timothy picked up his walking stick to leave – tomorrow, she would go to that small cupboard in the dining room, find the bottles of pills there, and empty all of their contents into her mouth.

WALLS AND BORDERS
Ssekandi R Sseguja

The Jaguar Bus pulled up by the sides of Immigration offices at Katuna border post in Kabale District. Nancy, who was seated at the rear, got up from her seat as the bus *turn-boy* ordered everyone to make haste. She was now closer to home. She had replayed this scene in her mind countless times in the past months. As she stepped outside the bus, she felt her heels dig into the damp wet mud. Kabale was a cold place and she felt the cold bite to the bone.

"Next please," the immigration officer called out to an absented-minded Nancy. The man right behind her shoveled her out of the way and took to the clearing desk. She heard a lady behind her chant some words in Kinyarwanda; she did not understand what she was saying but she could sense impatience and irritation in her tone. Kinyarwanda was supposed to be her language, it hurt to know that she could not understand it.

Nancy headed towards the Rwandan side. She was a few metres away from crossing over - *home*. In her mind, she toyed with the feeling of being on the other side. The border, like a point of transformation, ceased to be just a yellow line separating two sovereignties. It was the difference between home and *that place* back there, a place she had decided to leave.

Nancy and her family left Rwanda in 1994 during the genocide. Her mother had told her on several occasions how their family had been separated and some of her relatives killed. She had told her of their old family home in Nyamirambo. She always said it was cozier than the little shack where they lived in South Western Uganda. A place where Nancy had never felt at home because of the way her people were treated.

From as far back as she could remember, life had been different for her, haunted by the past of her people. In school, people would always ask once they knew that she was of Rwandan descent, which of the two tribes she belonged to. She had to be either Hutu or Tutsi. This made her feel like a subject of study most times. It hurt to be associated with a culture and tradition she knew little about.

Now on the Rwandan side, Nancy got back into the bus and began the last drive to Kigali city. She had heard so much about Kigali; tales of how it was probably the cleanest city in Africa. Some people even said that Kigali was like *Europe*. She was told that in Kigali *boda boda*, the famous crazy motorcyclists, were not allowed to carry more than one passenger and this was something she could not imagine!

Through her window, she could see the steep terrain of the countryside. Farmed hills of green, and livestock, symbolizing the peace that now reigned in this land. Her mother had told her of their big farmland in Bugesera. She was told that as a child, she used to like going to the farm to eat guavas. She now smiled to herself as she felt the sensation of nostalgia. Being here had always been her dream and she was elated the day had finally come.

Nyabugogo Bus Park is the place where all buses coming from Uganda stop. Nancy was finally home! As passengers dismounted, she took the opportunity to take in her environment. The quiet, calm landscape of Kigali at night. Numerous streetlights shone with a deep yellow richness, giving the city a romantic disposition.

At this moment, right there in the safety of the cozy bus, she felt the whole world pause as she spiritually connected to this place that for generations had harbored her ancestors. Deep down, she felt butterflies flutter and she smiled. How good it felt to be home.

Uri gusohoka muri bus mada?

Nancy was brought back to reality by the *turn-boy's* call. From the look on his face, she could tell he had been standing there for a long time. Reluctantly, she gathered her bag and headed out. She was immediately swarmed by a fleet of motorcyclists chanting phrases in Kinyarwanda. Fear gripped her as she realised that she was going to have trouble communicating with her people. Yet again, she felt the shame of not knowing her language. For some reason, she felt that this was the missing link to her *home* dream.

Before Nancy set off from Uganda, she had had a bitter argument with her mother who was against her desire to go *home*. That morning, Nancy had pressed her for the reason.

"You should just listen to me!" she had replied, throwing her hands in the air frantically and pacing around the compound. "If you cannot tell me, then I am going to find out by myself"

She could tell that her mother was not comfortable discussing the topic, but she had her mind made up and she set off.

"Please do not go Nancy!" she pleaded amidst wails and tears.

Nancy hated hurting her mother but in that moment, she felt she had to break through from the confines of her mother's supposed protection.

Where to Madam?

For the first time, Nancy felt the hopelessness of her adventure. Truthfully, she did not know where exactly she was going.

Nyamirambo.

The cyclist began the ride while muttering more words in Kinyarwanda. Nancy tells him in English that she does not understand Kinyarwanda. He asks her if she speaks French and she shakes her head. The cyclists smiles shyly and shrugs his shoulders. Nancy knows that he wanted to know where exactly in Nyamirambo she was going. Deep down she wishes he knew her story.

They take the first turn after the Bus Park and the motorcycle puffs as they climb a hill. Along the way, they bypass heavily armed soldiers patrolling the streets. Nancy wonders why this peaceful place should be heavily guarded. The motorbike now reaches a busy area, it is a street of bars and numerous people are out on the streets at this time of the night. Nancy watches in amusement as the cyclist goes a little slower, as if reading her mind.

The cyclist stopped. Nancy could barely understand him but knew that this had to be the end point for Nyamirambo. She got off and handed him some Rwandese francs. She then walked off as though she knew where she was going. She heard the cyclist call her back and she turned to see him following her. He muttered some words and handed her money as he smiled. She was amazed by his kindness. Back where she lived, such an act of kindness to an ignorant traveller would not be done. Were all the people here this nice?

Now that she was in Nyamirambo, Nancy felt the futility of her actions. Where was she going next? She had no idea where their *big house* was. She did not know whom to ask at this time of the morning. Fear began to creep in as she imagined the worst. She decided to find a lodging for the remainder of the early morning as she waited for people to start the day.

Rwanda was an hour behind Uganda and she was surprised that it was bright outside even though it was supposedly 4am! She walked towards a neon sign. *Dreams Guest House.* Nancy walked in, her body weighed down by the fatigue of the long journey. Luckily for her, the receptionist knew a little English and she was able to book herself into a room. Once inside, she locked her door and collapsed onto the bed.

Nancy must have slept for hours. She woke up to the sound of loud music outside. As she attempted to open her eyes, the sun glared through her window, blinding her. Her mind fumbled as she tried to remember where she was. She then instinctively jumped out of the bed; as though she had seen a snake in it. She rushed for her handbag, got out her phone and checked the time. It was midday! She had no idea she would sleep for this long. She felt a sudden desire to rush. Her plan was to get to her home as soon as she could. After her shower, she was now fresh and ready to go.

Luckily, the girl who had checked her in was still at the reception. Nancy paid her and then asked to be directed to her home. The girl asked where exactly her home was and Nancy fumbled with her bag, got out a rough paper on which she had written a name.

Mr. Sibomana.

That was the name of her father or, at least the name her mother had always used to refer to the man who supposedly fathered her. Growing up, it had always been taboo to ask her mum about this part of her life. She always changed moods when Nancy attempted to ask questions about her origins. The receptionist was now talking to her ...

Sibomana? Which Sibomana?

Nancy was startled by her tone. Why was she sounding alarmed? She got out her piece of paper and read the name again, making sure she made no mistake.

Felicitus Sibomana.

'Why are you asking about Felicitus Sibomana?' The girl asked, making Nancy really very uncomfortable now. From the look on her face, Nancy could tell there was some mystery about the name. The receptionist asked to be excused as she went to call her manager. Nancy sat down and waited uncomfortably.

After what seemed like the longest wait in her life, the receptionist returned with two men. She watched them conferring in hushed tones. The receptionist stole glances at Nancy and occasionally pointed towards her. The two men finally approached.

Come with us ...

From the way they spoke, Nancy knew that she had no choice. She got up and followed them to the truck outside. They sped her through the city until they reached a house with a high gate. It was heavily guarded and Nancy now began to shiver. Was this a kidnapping? She motioned towards one of the men to ask him but one glance at his face and she remained silent. They led her inside the house and ordered her to sit down.

How do you know Sibomana?

Sibomana is my father.

Where is he?

Now this was getting scary because the men were getting increasingly aggressive.

I do not know where he is.

Nancy was told that Sibomana was a hunted fugitive in this country. That her father was one of the perpetrators of the 1994 genocide in which thousands of innocent people had been massacred. She was asked to state his whereabouts or else face the consequences.

I do not know where he is.

Nancy was crying. This was too much information for her. She now understood why her mother hated talking about the subject. She could not believe that the blood of a murderer flowed through her. She pleaded with the men and told them of how shehad grown up with her mother and did not know anything about her father.

Captain, put her in the cells. When she is ready to talk, she will be brought out.

The captain dragged her down a long dark corridor and then turned left. She was hit by a nasty stench as she was led to what appeared to be a stretch of metallic doors. He stopped at one of them and pulled out a bunch of keys. He then opened it and tossed Nancy inside. She landed on something long and hard, heard the door close and then broke into sobs.

Shut up you bitch!

Nancy got up defensively, startled to hear another voice inside the cell. Her eyes now accustomed to the dark, she noticed a sea of faces looking at her. She saw five tired faces of women who from their physical appearance seemed to have been in the cell for a while. They looked hopeless and in pain. The stench inside was so strong that Nancy held her nose.

Do not worry, you will get used to it after days.

The voice came from an old woman in the corner. She looked calm and more composed than the rest of the inhabitants. Locked up in this cell with strange faces, Nancy felt trapped. Her dream of a good homecoming suddenly vanished as she realized that she was now a prisoner. She thought of her mother back in Uganda and the grave look on her face as she left that morning. Why had she not told her the truth? Nancy began weeping silently, her body rocking with both fatigue and fear. Trapped in the strong cell walls, she felt that feeling again; the feeling she always felt when people in Uganda pointed at her and said "Banyarwanda!"

Was she meant to forever live in walls?

LONGLISTED STORIES

DAY AFTER TOMORROW
Paul Ugbede

In the year 2032, exactly two months after President Makari heard clearly from God that Abuja should bomb Washington on the day of the blood moon, I heard the knock. Bekky was sleeping on my lap and I think she heard the knock before I did. She was already at the edge of the sofa, her eyes, two large saucers, her lips, a badly written 'O'. Those lips always got me and I wanted to push my breast in her mouth. She liked that, she called it impromptu harassment. She would suck at my nipple and clasp her long fingers around my arse.

The knock came again, this time sharp, brittle and hard on my chest. Mama was sitting on that single chair by the window, not flinching, her face chiseled out of stone. That moment, I knew I shouldn't have told her.

'Why?' I asked her. She just stared above my head, above my question. I wanted to ask why she had to call the *Soja Allah* and not her friend who was supposed to get us the train tickets to Ghana. Instead, I focused on how much I looked like her, how much of her long hair I had ... How much of her dark skin colour ... How much we had shared for twenty-three years.

'Why, Mama?'

'You need a cure Hajarat ... ' Her thin fingers clamped on the edges of her seat. 'Root Camp is for your own good.'

The door crashed open and they spilled in. Twelve *Soja Allah* - their blue uniforms giving a sad hue to the dark room. *'Salam Alekum, Salam Alekum!'*

Bekky dashed to the door but two of the men grabbed her mid stride and pushed her to the floor. She fighting and screaming, they pushing and shouting *Allahu Akbar! Allahu Akbar!* I felt sorry for her, hating myself for not listening to her, for thinking that my mother was different from hers, that she would understand and help us escape.

Her scream clutched my intestines, turning them round and round in a tight knot. My knees buckled but strong arms held me and pushed me to the floor. A sharp needle pierced through my neck. Bekky's scream now sounded like a dull drum and Mama was now a fiery ghost. I think she was saying 'I love you Hajarat' but I was not sure as I was any longer in the room.

* * *

42

'Stand up! Idiot! Nyanch banger! Toto licker! Up on your feet!' The voice sounded from somewhere inside my head. Gradually it became real, a male voice. I scrambled to my feet and bumped my head against something.

'Bekky!' I called softly, peering through the darkness. 'I'm here!' Her hand found mine and she held me. Her fingers were cold and she was trembling. 'Where are we?'

Strong light hit my face. I squinted and held Bekky's hand tightly. The light left my face and my eyes followed it. We were in the back of a truck and we were not alone. The truck was filled with young boys and girls.

'Oya bigin come out one by one!' The male voice barked again. 'One single line! See them! Nyanch banger! Toto licker! *Gerrout!*' Bekky came down after me. Her hand found mine again and I held her. A stick hit my hand, making me wince in pain. I quickly let go of Bekky's hand.

'Dirty girl!' The voice barked. 'You still wan lick toto for Root Camp? Oya forward *marsh!*'

How many were we? Fifty? A hundred? I didn't really know, but we all marched for a long time, through tall shadows of caricature trees hugging the dark night. Once in a while, the male voice hit someone on the head with his stick and shouted, 'why you dey look me? Why you dey look me? You wan fuck my nyanch? *You wan fuck my nyanch?*'

We came to a high-fenced building with a mighty blue gate and bright lights. There were blue uniforms everywhere.

'Straight to the gate! Straight to the gate!'

Root Camp comprised two tall white warehouses with little windows high up in the sky. We were huddled between the two buildings, trying to melt into one another, trying to get away from the *Soja Allah* who were moving around us, ogling us, weighing us with their eyes, touching our breasts, squeezing our buttocks. Bekky was seven girls behind me. Was she limping on her left leg?

A tall woman walked briskly from one of the buildings towards us. She was so tall that her uniform hung on her like a question mark. Her fair face reminded me of onions and she had an oily smile. The men quickly stood to attention.

'Welcome to Root Camp, God's healing Project!' she said huskily. 'I am Aunty Caro, spiritual head. All the men please go to the right and all the women to the left.'

No movement.

'Una no dey hear? Toto lickers to the left, nyanch bangers to the right!' That now familiar voice barked. Aunty Caro glanced at him, her smile not wavering.

We quickly made two lines. The male line was shorter than the female line.

'All the males follow this man and all the females, follow me.' She turned round and headed back towards the building from whence she had come. A blue uniform opened the metal door and we all went in. It closed with a loud clang behind our backs. The building was in darkness and a light came on.

'All of you will sleep here.' Aunty Caro's oily smile became wider. 'This is the last night you shall spend together for the next six months. This night is called silent night because whatever you do, God will not be watching you.' She turned around and disappeared with the light.

Through the darkness, we began to search each other out, creating pockets of worlds within the walls. I found Bekky and she held me tightly.

'It's going to be alright.' I stroked her corn ridge.

Silence.

Someone was kissing someone in the darkness, a noisy, slippery, sloppiness.

'Are we really sick?' Bekky's whispered question scratched my silent mind.

Are we really sick? It was a painful question, one I had never thought about. The freshness of it bled down my heart, trailing the crevices of my mind for answers, answers that were not really there. Are we really sick?

Bekky fell asleep, curled in my arms. Capsules of snores rose from different corners. The kissing was still going on, the slippery sloppiness accentuated by gentle moans.

I did not know how many minutes I'd closed my eyes for before the scream tore through the night. It came again, a loud soul-rendering wail. Everyone must have heard it too because the snores were gone, kisses stopped.

'What is that?' Bekky asked. Her fear visible in her question. She was sitting up now.

It was the scream of a woman and it was coming from somewhere inside her, from somewhere under her bile, somewhere in the nest of her life. How old was she? Twenty? Forty? Can one tell age through pain? Does pain have an age?

'It will stop soon. Try not to think about it,' I said.

But it did not stop, it kept on and on, torturing our senses, tearing through our souls until it became a part of the night, a block in the wall...a thought in our minds. By the time I found sleep, the scream was in my dream and this time, it was Aunty Caro screaming in my ears through her oily smile.

* * *

'Get up! Get up!'

Morning had come unnoticed. It came with three guards, Aunty Caro and her oily smile. The morning light lent a little moisture to her onion face. There was a pile of white clothes on the floor.

Aunty Caro's voice was a husky blue. 'The world out there belongs to God's servant, President Makari. But Root Camp belongs to *me*. After God, it is President Makari, then me, in that order. Your parents don't know where you are so if you want to get back to them, you must cooperate with me. Is that alright?'

'Yes Aunty Caro,' we chorused.

'What is happening to you is evil. For a woman to have feelings for another woman is evil. For a man to have feelings for another man is evil, but God will heal you. There were others here before you and they have been healed and gone home. God will heal all of you!'

'There was a scream last night ...' I said though it was meant to be a question.

'The scream ... It is coming from those undergoing the spiritual therapy. It is the only music you'll hear in Root Camp, so get used to it.' She stared at me, a spark in her eyes. I turned away. I knew what that spark meant.

'Each of you will be allotted a room. Please get into these clothes and enjoy your stay at Root Camp.' As she left, she threw a glance at me. Her oily smile was beginning to make me feel queasy.

My room was a smaller version of where we slept last night, nothing except for an empty bucket. The odour of urine was masked with *Izal*. I went to the corner of the room, away from the bucket and sat down. As I examined my new white overalls, my door opened. A *Soja Allah* pulled me up by my arm and pushed me out of the room. Still holding my arm, he dragged me to a door at the end of the hall. He knocked, shoved me into a room and closed the door behind me.

The room was furnished with a red bed and a red rug.

Aunty Caro stood in a corner of the room, smiling. 'So this is the intelligent girl that asked a question?' She was close to me now, her hot breath fanning my face.

I took a step backwards and was against the door. She smelled like a newly washed cat. Her eyes undressed me, her onion face overwhelmed me.

'Intelligent and beautiful,' she whispered into my ear. 'You're mine. I chose you.'

Then she kissed me. She kissed like an angry bat. I was dazed, not from the kiss but from the fact that we were in Root Camp, the house of God and this was Aunty Caro our healer.

She peeled off her uniform and stood before me, naked. Her breasts looked like two deflated egos.

'Suck my breasts.' She threw her head back, eyes closed. 'Squeeze them.'

I squeezed.

'Harder.'

She let out a little moan. 'Harder, you bitch!'

My hands were numb with pain but she kept urging me to squeeze. I was sweating now and the pain was surging through my brain.

'Squeeze harder, bastard!' she shouted.

'My hands...'

She gave me a sharp slap, cutting my sentence. 'I say squeeze!' Her eyes were animated and the oily smile had melted into molten desire.

And I squeezed, crying now. The more I cried, the more she moaned until I crashed on the bed in painful exhaustion. 'Please!' I cried.

She was on me, tearing at my overalls. Her head went between my thighs. Her tongue felt like a slimy snake darting in, oozing venom. As the snake probed deeper, I thought of Bekky, of what she was doing, of whether she was still limping on one leg. She came back the following night. And every other night. The cycle became familiar; she would come in, satisfy herself, flop into a thunderous snore and by first dawn, she would rap on the door thrice and be gone, leaving me scratched and broken. I began to dread the nights, the sound of her footsteps, her onion face, her oily smile, her touch ... What kept me sane was that scream.

I selfishly longed for it. It was better than Aunty Caro's moan. I noticed it was not just one scream. There were many of them, from different girls, each one with its own octave…each one with its own story. I could tell when a scream was repeating a cycle, when a scream died. I envied them, those screamers. At least they could scream. I longed to be a part of that scream too, to scream my heart out and stop myself from falling into darkness.

She noticed I was dying silently and I think she was genuinely concerned. 'You can ask anything and I'll grant it,' she said one morning after she had woken up and was putting on her uniform.

'I want to see my friend.' It tumbled out of my mouth.

Her oily smile slipped a little but it was back again.

'Bekky?' My eyes opened wide.

She smiled. 'You're surprised? It is my duty to know about my patients.' She looked at me. 'Tonight.' And she was gone.

The thought of seeing Bekky after four months overwhelmed me. Had she grown lean? Was she eating at all? That night, I took my bath and waited on the bed, wearing the gown Aunty Caro had bought for me. For the first time in four months, I unstrapped my desire from the window where I had hung it and put it on.

At night, the door opened and she was there, a little frail, a little smaller.

'Bekky!'

She held me close. Sniffing my neck, letting out a soft sigh. I missed her so much, her lips, her eyes, her hands …

'You are living better than the rest of us,' she said, when we sat on the bed.

'Aunty Caro …'

'I know … We all know … We hear it every night.' She stared at me. 'I was angry at first but I understand now.'

I wanted to say I was sorry but I was looking at her instead, thinking of how thin she had become, how distant her eyes were …

'She told me I have not gone for therapy because of you … Thank you.' She quickly stood up and was out of her overalls. Bekky was gaunt and her fair skin had become white.

'Stop staring and come here. We have this night alone.' My gown slipped down my legs. A cold sadness hung somewhere inside my soul. Have we finally lost each other?

When her mouth found mine, I realised this was what I

47

wanted … Who I wanted. The tension between us melted with the kiss and we were moaning, squeezing, climbing higher and higher … Then the door opened and they were upon us, blue uniforms shouting *Innalillahi!* in horror. We quickly disengaged, screaming in fear as they dragged us up. Aunty Caro stood in the doorway, smiling her oily smile.

'Have you ever seen what makes those girls scream?' She asked me, her oily smile glistening. 'You will come and watch.'

They dragged Bekky along the corridor. She was screaming and calling on me to help her. I ran after Aunty Caro, begging, crying but she just kept smiling her oily smile. The therapy room had a single six-spring bed and the *Soja Allah* threw Bekky onto it. Eight men crowded the room and began to remove their clothes. Bekky struggled, thrashing her legs in the air and screaming in fear. Two blue uniforms held her legs and spread them wide.

The first man thrust into her, a long, vengeful thrust. I had never heard such screams before, loud animal screams that were tearing into the night, wrenching my brain apart. I was crying and begging, lunging towards Bekky, but powerless against the hands holding me. Aunty Caro kept smiling. When the sixth man was halfway, Bekky passed out. But they continued.

Becky came to and started screaming again, a cow-like scream that seemed to ooze from the pores of her skin. After an eternity, the men left and another eight entered. I threw up. By the time they had finished, Bekky was lifeless.

They buried her that night in a fenced-out yard in Root Camp, among thousands of other graves. That same night, Aunty Caro came to me.

'I don't share, you should know that,' she said, still smiling. As her snake went in and out of my thighs, I thought about all those graves at Root Camp, all those people who have 'been healed and gone home.' Did they wear white hand gloves? I thought all dead people wore white hand gloves so they could become angels in heaven. My father wore white hand gloves when he was buried. Bekky did not wear any.

Aunty Caro lay face down on the bed snoring louder than ever. I watched her back rising and falling and I made up my mind. This is the night I must kill her. I had thought about it every night, how I was going to do it, what can kill her faster than sixteen penises.

I stood up and put on her uniform. It was a little tight on

the bust but it fitted. I rapped thrice on the door and it opened. I walked down the corridor, past open gates, past saluting blue uniforms saying, *Allah ya taimake Makari!*

Outside, I paused to breathe in the fresh night air and stared up at the sky. The blood moon was up. The sign President Makari was waiting for. Everyone was chanting *Allah ya taimake Makari.*

I ran through the forest, away from Root Camp, from the chanting, from Aunty Caro … Mama. To somewhere? Anywhere? Nowhere? I didn't know. I just kept running.

It will be a while before the blood moon goes down. President Makari will direct his nuclear missile at Washington, his face to us … And nothing will ever be the same.

DR LAWANSON
Wale Lawal

5th November 1994
Dr. Abọsẹde Betty Lawanson
Lawanson Court
17 Albert Street
Apapa, Lagos.

Dear Rotimi Jr./Betty,

A little girl stopped by my clinic earlier this afternoon. Actually, she didn't stop by. What I ought to have written was she was wheeled into my clinic. I asked for her age, I was told fifteen. I asked for her name, I was told Bọsẹ - oh, how I nearly wept because we were namesakes! I have never been able to tolerate my namesakes. I regret that they are never nearly like me; that not only do they share my name, they also have access to life's universal free will and use their free will to do bad things. Things I do not like. Things like getting pregnant at the age of fifteen.but what is peculiar about this particular Bọsẹ is how often I have seen her since 1964; never growing, frozen fifteen; since the 5th of November: the day I first treated myself.

I call it treating myself, and perhaps you will understand why. Perhaps you will not. Don't worry. I will be neither surprised nor disappointed.

A few years ago, I was at an award ceremony in Yaba. I'd rather start there. The ceremony was organised by the Nigerian Women in Medicine Association (NWIMA), over which I presided at the time. Nigerians have a strange affinity for acronyms and it just occurred to me to wonder why we pronounce NWIMA as if it is an Igbo name. I was awarded Doctor of the Year and a grant of thirty thousand dollars, in recognition of my research on what is commonly known today as In Vitro Fertilisation and my attempts to reduce the outbreak of Vesicovaginal Fistula (VVF) in the North. My husband, you will know him, the spare and sweet Dr. Rotimi Lawanson, heard someone say at the ceremony that she was certain I was going to be profiled by The Herald. My profile was to be captioned "Africa's Most Prominent Obstetrician".

The interview did happen. It began at 8 a.m. Sharp. Nigerians are naturally tardy but everyone knows The Herald is a standard newspaper. In fact, it was the best newspaper the 80s had to offer. At 7:30, the bell rang twice and Clifford the steward opened the door. I was sat with Rotimi in the dining area. We were having breakfast. A rather nebbish, young man entered the room. He was bespectacled and had terrible deportment, but spoke remarkably fine English. We invited him to sit and have some breakfast with us. However, the man pretended as though he hadn't been offered a meal and began to whistle. Mr. Lekan was his name. Lekan Wright. What terrible mannerisms he had! Eventually, to put us out of the misery of his whistling, Rotimi decided to offer him some tea. This time, he accepted to join us albeit with an effusive display of gratitude.

From the dining area, we moved to the parlour. There, I was to begin my interview. I sat by a vase containing the most beautiful magnolias and Rotimi made his way upstairs.

"Rotimi dear, won't you stay?" I asked him.

"Stay? No my dear, I wouldn't want to ruin the moment but I shall read all about it in the papers," he said. We had been married over twenty years and yet he was unchanging in his sweetness.

My everlasting ixora.

"So," said the interviewer. He caught my attention by clearing his throat. What a ghastly man he was. "Africa's most prominent obstetrician . . . " he began.

"Oh please," I interposed, laughing bashfully.

"Is a woman?" he added and I laughed but only out of courtesy.

"Of course she is. I mean, the nature of the profession alone is already what gives me the edge."

"As I said before, I won't take much of your time. Pictures and your biography will take up most of the spread. How did you become interested in obstetrics? Were your parents doctors?"

"Far from it! My father was a pastor and my mother was a teacher. And so I suppose at an early age, I was inclined towards an academic life. But I've always drawn inspiration from my own body. You know how as a child, you fall down a flight of stairs and

51

there's a wound in your leg and you stare at it for a little while – I became curious about my own body rather early."

"And your parents encouraged you I would think?"

"I don't know whether to call it encouragement but when I was at school, what was fashionable among the other girls was Nursing. I remember my mother wanted me to become a nurse. 'All the girls going to England are studying Nursing,' she said. My father wasn't too interested in me. We were eight children, still eight, and I am the sixth. He focused on the boys and my mother focused on the girl."

"And why wouldn't you choose Nursing then? Since you say it was fashionable."

"It simply wasn't the best choice for me. I wanted to do more, and I'm sure the world is glad that I'm not a nurse."

The man laughed and afterwards, shifted in his chair. I knew the next question. I had been expecting it. I didn't dread it, however. I had been asked the question far too many times before.

"So do you have any children?"

"No," is the brusque response I always give but this interviewer was persistent and so I thought I'd be a little cheeky and try to beat an interviewer at his own game. "Well, my husband and I simply don't like children very much."

"But you're an obstetrician, surely you must –" "Once again, Mr. Wright, you have proven that you do not understand the nature of my profession. That I don't have or like children does not mean I am incapable of being a competent obstetrician. Let's not cast a hapless net in search of irrelevant sources of validation. I am good at what I do – in fact, I am brilliant at what I do, simply because I focus a great deal on the women giving birth to these children. Society will have you think only of the end and neglect the means. It's a sickening Nigerian mentality. "

"I'm sorry if I . . . "

"No, you can be sorry after I finish. And I want this in the paper. Have you looked through my research or followed my work in the North? I have always stressed that while children are a 'bundle of joy', the women bearing these children are equally if not more important. So my choosing not to have children, so I can dedicate my life to ensuring other women can have healthier and safer childbirths is enough validation for me."

"And how does your husband take it? Off the record."

"Do you hear him complaining? He himself is a passionate doctor and we are both equally passionate about what we do. So passionate that I am afraid if we had a child, we simply wouldn't be able to cope."

We capered around this subject for several hours, until we rounded up the interview and he rose to leave. It was yet another interview in which I had been asked the question about children. Of course, there are rumours. Once, I even heard a member of NWIMA whisper to another member that I "may be barren". It will surprise you, the result, when society happens upon even the most educated women. And so I had to be barren or a witch or an apaọmọjẹ (a child-devourer). Nothing I had never heard before. And even after my dazzling profile in The Herald, I was still all of those things, which have never been more to me than words.

Hours after the end of the interview, a photographer arrived with an entourage of three. I was convinced the photo session would never end. It ended in the evening and I settled into a cool bath. As he always does, Rotimi filled the house with the music of the grand piano downstairs. Chopin's nocturnes had never sounded more enrapturing and yet they evoked a poignant reminder of the things I had said about children during the interview that morning.

Rotimi did want a child. In fact, while at university, we often spoke about the family we would raise together. What a shock it was when, a few years later, I told him that I did not want children. Oh, how he had been gingering himself for the rearing of the head, while I grew to extremely dread that very moment. My fears began in April 1954, when a fifteen-year-old girl was rushed into the General Hospital in Marina where I worked. I was twenty-eight at the time but I was already on my way to becoming quite the seasoned obstetrician. The girl was a victim of sexual assault. She had only managed to hide the assault from her family for so long. A pregnant womb soon reveals the secret by itself. Two nurses wheeled her down the corridor and from behind a jalousie I watched the operation. For the first time ever in my career as a doctor, I felt a certain chill. A fright. It dared me to scream but I would not dare be courageous. The girl was so gaunt and her cervix was too small. I could not bear to watch the entire operation. She died was all I stole later, from the private gossip of two nurses.

"But the child lived. It was either her or the child." Then in July, I became pregnant and lost the baby as soon as I found out. Two years later, in November, I became pregnant again. By now, Rotimi and I were well into our marriage but had agreed to put our respective medical disciplines ahead of children. We had a dream to set up our own practice. The taller, concrete building adjacent to our house is the result of that dream. You see, pregnancy used to drive me into a brief spell of distress. A swirl of madness, so to speak. Women are always told that pregnancies ought to incite some sort of motherly instinct but if mine ever came, it came far too late. At first, I did want a child. I felt so terrible that I could not handle something so natural; that I could not do what so many women can so easily do. The sensations of pregnancy came at me in the form of nightmares. I would wake up in a pool of sweat. My chest would be beating faster than my feet can run. My insides would contort into a whorl. I felt infested and sick and that was how I often discovered I was pregnant. And I was never wrong.

The first time I aborted a pregnancy, Rotimi and I sought out a doctor recommended by a friend of a friend. We were madly in love but too young and too poor to start a family. I was only twenty-four and he, twenty-two. The doctor was a stroppy middle-aged man, who wouldn't touch me unless he had been paid. And what we paid forty pounds for was the operation. It did not buy the eschewal of the doctor's scathing judgement. The operation was very hush-hush. The only other person who knows about it is dead. I didn't kill him. He died of old age. And for his sake, to protect his memory, I shall end this apostrophe here.

As one would expect, the next time I became pregnant, I paid a visit to a woman. A female nurse: a jittery Marcia McBroom doppelgänger who hid avian features behind a pair of red wing-tipped glasses. She could not be serious, I thought to myself. She was far too self-conscious to be a nurse. The woman called herself a professional but she was so terrified of touching me. Of all things to do, she held on to a rosary and prayed before summoning the pluck to operate on me. But she did operate on me and without criticism I might add (although she had a perversion for small talk).

By this time, I had begun a slow ascent career-wise. Rotimi and I had not started our own practice yet but I especially was beginning to receive tremendous acclaim for the work I was doing in the North. Nobody had thought to see the lives of those prematurely pregnant girls as urgent and important, but I bit that gun and braved the bullet. The underside of this steady rise to fame was that I eventually had to part ways with Linda my religiose nurse. I feared that she might soon discover who I was. I remember distinctly, thinking: "Why, I'm an obstetrician, why not take matters into my own hands?"

So I did.

Both the doctor and the nurse had operated on me with steel rods but it would have been terribly impractical, not to mention unsafe and foolish for me to ever consider conducting a physical operation on myself. I had not been pregnant in a while, but I had the fortune of my medical activities in Kano. I was part of a somewhat covert group of scientists who were at the onset of developing a ground-breaking formula that would greatly mitigate the horrors faced not only by the northern girls but also by female victims of sexual assault in general. We called it a Sleeper. Can you imagine? Something you drink, that makes the pregnancy just fizzle away? They thought we were mad. Some said we were challenging God. But I believe we were the hand of God, correcting the foul habits of man. Rape is not an act, it happens so often that it ought to be classified as a habit.

The next time I became pregnant, I felt it attack me without restraint. It tore me from sleep. Rotimi slept through it all. I kept a few bottled Sleepers in my wardrobe and a cap-full is all I needed to be able to sleep. I'll admit over the years, it became a sort of game. A challenge: nature against Dr. Lawanson. And how I grew to enjoy teasing nature! Sometimes, I would wait to see how far I could withstand my fears before running to my wardrobe. But never had I let my stomach swell or reveal my womb's secret. Not until the night before the first time Bọsẹ was brought to my clinic.

"I've seen her before," I said to a nurse. Indeed I had. I had seen Bọsẹ ten years ago in 1954!

Bọsẹ was taken into a ward and for the first time, a girl died in my clinic. What a horror it was! Rotimi and I had just started our practice and it almost caused a scandal. Rotimi believed in doppelgängers. I had never known such people even existed until that very night. Of the two of us, he was the more widely read. He was so knowledgeable that at that point in my life consulting him might very well have been a pavlovian response.

"They probably just look alike," he said.

"They had the same name and age," I protested.

"We live in a world of infinite possibilities," he said and I kissed him on his leathery forehead.

Before he even fell asleep, it occurred to me that the night before, I had succumbed to my fears and swilled a Sleeper. I saw Bọsẹ again in 1974. It was again the 5th of November. Again she was wheeled into the clinic but unlike the last time, she and the nurses disappeared after sharply turning left off the corridor. Yet not unlike the last time, I had found solace in a bottle of Sleeper the night before.

It was ten years later, in July 1984, that I was awarded Doctor of the Year. By this time, Bọsẹ seemed to linger constantly in the marshes of my peripheral vision but I kept her a secret. I saw her again when I walked into the ceremony. I saw her again when I stood up to receive my award. I saw her everywhere. And then the sharpest headache interrupted my acceptance speech. Rotimi had to rush me home. It was on our way out that he heard the rumour about The Herald. And after the profile, I resigned. It was the most dazzling farewell to a career ever given. I became a celebrity of sorts. From time to time, I still visited the clinic. However, during the years thereafter, I spent most of my time, scouring universities for promising medical students. I gave speeches. I lectured women. "It all comes with being president," I was told. And one cannot so easily resign from being the President of NWIMA. I was rounding up my visit to the clinic this afternoon when a little girl stopped by. I hadn't seen her in while.

She was being wheeled around the clinic. Her breathing was desperate. She sat with her legs apart on the wheelchair.

Her head was tilted to one side. Her hair resembled a cloud of black smoke. Bọsẹ was breastfeeding a baby. I asked for her age. Fifteen.

The girl was a victim of sexual assault. Nobody had escorted her to the hospital. Nobody had come in search of her. I took the baby from her and slowly, began to walk away.

"Naomi, don't worry, she's the owner of the clinic," I heard a nurse say to Bọsẹ.

"Boy or a girl?" I thought to myself.

Rotimi has always wanted a boy. We spoke about these things while we were young and madly in love. I, on the other hand, once wanted a girl. A beautiful rose. I grew up in a house with seven brothers. I have decided to wait for Rotimi to come home. We'll check which baby you are. Together.

Yours Reluctantly,

Dr. Lawanson

FIRE IN THE NIGHT
Myke Mwale

The cold wind pipes across the hovering jacarandas, forcing the leaves to dance into submission. Xoliswa has lit a fire under a huge tree at our usual spot, at the corner of Mabhena and Mpondo Street. We are squatting around it and my spine tingles with warmth. I like the fire and I always wish I could squat around it for hours in the night, just as we did around Gogo's fireplace. The fire crackles as Xoliswa turns over one of the small logs and prods the young embers, sending sparks into the cold air. The crispy night quickly douses them and they fizzle into the darkness without a trace. I scuttle back away from the fire before it scalds my shins and thighs. Agitated butterflies churn in my lower stomach as if it is my first night here. They always do this every time, every night. It is as if I want to go to the toilet but I recognize this false alarm. Xoliswa is noisily chewing her bubble gum, pretending she is not nervous. When we arrived here there were five of us, but the other three have already gone into the night.

A car slithers towards us and we lift our heads. You can tell when somebody is driving past. You can also tell when they are perusing the shadows. The headlights beam, casting us into dazzling light. We both look away cursing under our breath. The problem is when the lights are so bright like that you cannot easily tell if it is a police car or not. By the time you see the light bar on top of the car it is too late and scurrying into the darkness is futile. The car gets closer to the fire. The window is pulled down and I can see a dark figure driving a red car. Not surprisingly, he drives past and parks about a stone's throw away.

"The idiot! Whom does he want?" I stand up.

"Let him come here Anele. The ear does not go to the finger," Xoliswa quips, still squatting. We both chuckle.

"It is not the finger that needs scratching but the ear," I respond and Xoliswa's laugh slices the stony night.

Cars that had been trailing the red car pass by, but the driver does not come out of his car. He sits there with the engine idling; the quivering exhausts farting into the raw night. Another

58

car passes from the opposite direction but the driver is not interested. The driver of the red car hoots lightly. We stare into the hissing fire as if we cannot see or hear him. The raucous dog from one of the big houses along Mpondo Street speeds to the fence to investigate. Its loud barks query the silent night. The red car is just parked there with its rear lights glowing like a pair of red traffic lights. Soon other dogs join in the yapping and snarling at the cold night.

"He is irritating me! Let me go and see who he wants," I say to Xoliswa.

My skirt clings tightly to my waist, threatening to expose my thighs to the cold air with every step. A draught howls behind me chasing plastics, papers and dry leaves across the dimly lit street. The butterflies in my stomach start fluttering again. I look back at Xoliswa and she is still squatting and looking at me with her back to the fire. I edge in closer to the driver's side. I can make out the figure of a man fiddling with his radio player. The cold air nibbles the back of my thighs and ears as I lean forward towards the car. He is a young, corpulent man, and he gawks at me with his mouth ajar like a fish as if it's me who wants it. He scans me from head to foot, lingering on my bare thighs and trying to peep behind me, as if searching for something on my back.

"How much?" he finally utters after guzzling a lump of saliva.

I wish he could be more specific. There is no secrecy about this and the night is not getting any warmer. "Single or whole package, what do you want?" I control my voice.

"I need a quick-quick," he murmurs, his eyes darting from the rear to the side view mirrors.

"70 Rands for a stub and 350 for the whole pack," I disclose.

Now that the price has been stated, I wait for the bargaining. He looks at me again for some time. Xoliswa is coughing. I steal a glance at her. She is now standing and looking at us. I feel like shouting at this ambivalent man.

"That is too much! Do you do everything?" His eyes scurry everywhere.

"Depends on what you mean by everything." I pull up

59

my collar to shield my ears from the cold. He checks on the rear view mirror again.

Men who start by asking whether you do everything are strange. They can make you do anything, even ineffable things.

"Can I have your fat friend there by the fire instead? I hope you do not mind?" he croaks as he strokes a beardy chin.

Xoliswa is looking at me with that asking look when I rejoin her at the fire. "And then?" she chirps!

I hate it when she talks like this. "He says he wants you," I state as I squat again closer to the fire. I shudder with relief as the heat from the flames caresses my arms and legs.

"Why me?" she retorts. I can see her grinning from the corner of my eye.

"He says he wants fat and you are fat!" I hiss at her but she is already walking towards the car.

She adjusts her hair before leaning towards the driver of the red car. She is still chewing her bubble gum. They talk for some time and she comes back. The dogs have stopped barking but I can see their silhouettes through the fences. It is as if they know our natural scents despite all the other scents smeared onto us; cigarette smoke, beer, after shave, sweat, chicken, marijuana, wine, groundnuts, anything.

"Hold on to this money that he has paid. I will collect it when I come back just now." She hands me 90 Rands.

I want to ask why the man gave her 90 Rands but she is already swaying her bottom as she trots to the car. It is pointless to ask anyway since Xoliswa always has her way with men. Maybe it is her tight mini skirt that makes them pay more. The other girls think it's the *muti* that her mother gave her. I tuck the money safely into my bra and watch the red car make a U-turn and disappear with her into the cold silent night. The air is colder and embraces my skin like a small wet towel so I shuffle, like a crab, closer to the fire.

A black cat tiptoes from the ill-lit Mabhena Street. It stops for a moment, its eyes glowing in the dim light as it glares at me. The hair at the back of my head tugs at its roots. The dogs are excited again and are whining and growling at this intruder. The cat canters across the road into a dark alley. I turn around just to make sure that I am alone around the fire. The fire is gradually dying so I revive its flames with some logs, twigs and a cardboard box. The logs hiss, smoke gushing from their cracked barks. Soon the appeased flames are dancing again in the night and squat there looking at the passing cars, waiting.

A car drones its way from Mpondo Street. Its headlights send shadows that scamper away on the fence opposite from where I am enjoying the fire. The car glides sluggishly through the chilly night. I stand up. The driver does not waste time and immediately stops the car at the same place where the previous car stopped. One could actually assume that it was a demarcated parking spot. He makes a gesture for me to come to his car with his hazards. I walk away from the fire towards the car.

"Where can I find the others?" he enquires, looking at me as if he is asking for loose change.

"Which others?" I demand.

He does not look at me this time, but continues to tap his steering wheel with his thick fingers. The engine is still running and there are empty beer bottles on the front seat.

"You know I have been drinking. When I am drunk, you know, I want real challenge," he mutters with an awkward smile. What on earth is he saying? I can hear the fire popping behind me. I am about to turn and go when he slurs sheepishly, "I want men. I am looking for young men." He grins. "It is cold you know!"

"Go straight down the road and take a short left. Continue on that road and you will see them." I mumble and gladly stroll back to the fire.

He gabbles something and revs the car back into the road. I smile to myself as I glare into the glowing embers. I hope that he does not come back for me when he doesn't find his young men. They often do that when they cannot find the men. They come begging and pleading with you, even offering to double or triple your price if they can go with you. The young men are often unlucky since most men are scared of being seen with them in their cars. Men are also wary of muggers posing as one of us. Many have lost their cars and their belongings and have only reported half of their stories to the police.

The dancing flames have subsided but the ligneous

embers are smouldering at the heart of the fire. If hell is like this, then I guess it must be real torture. If sins are like firewood that one heaps for oneself in the everlasting fires, will I be writhing in those fiery cinders with pain? I have been writhing in pain under the weight of countless men, many whose faces I vaguely recall when I walk the streets during the day. But then one cannot be certain with these things. At least this fire is warm and I can hear the engine of a car.

The car, playing loud music, approaches and when it is passing by the fire, the driver shouts something and hoots. The dogs bawl again. The bars and taverns are closing and I am hoping that someone comes by sooner, or else I will go home with nothing but Xoliswa's money. She is not yet back but I am not worried. Maybe she was dropped somewhere and picked up again by somebody. I will pass by her place at dawn and leave the money with her mother. It has happened many times before and she likewise would leave my money at my place with my grandmother if I were not there.

My eyelids are hefty. I do not carry a watch or cellphone with me but I know that it is early morning because it is getting colder. It is as if the cold is having its last chilling bite before dawn announces its arrival. It is still dark but I know that in three hours the speckled doves will start cooing when the crickets finally surrender with exhaustion. It was Gogo who told us when we were young, sitting around the fire, that it is the male cricket that chirps at night - to attract females. I was young then, a mere school-girl. I never imagined that I would stand by this street corner at night, around a fire, waiting, chirping in silence for my life, my child and Gogo.

The dogs from the house are growling. I know that there is somebody coming. I cannot see anybody in the dark but I know they can see me since I am squatting under the lamppost. The dogs begin barking. I can make out the form of a tall man in a trench coat walking towards me. I cannot see his face. I slowly stand upright, pulling my skirt down. People do not go for walks at this hour. As he approaches I can see that he is walking with a slight limp.

"Come with me!" the tall man blurts, still standing in the

shadows.

"Where are we going?" I probe.

"Are you coming or not? How much is it? Let's hurry it's almost dawn," he spits.

I state the price, adding a little bit more, hoping that it would dissuade him. To my disbelief he snorts in approval and starts walking away. I follow him, trying to keep up with his long strides. We walk silently in the piercing cold, past the eerie cemetery, the gloomy church, the oddly silent beer hall. The man just limps on. He does not even hum or cough.

He finally stops in the freshly burnt veld near a footpath, under the thorny acacia trees. I have been here myriad times before. What is it about these trees? I move on to another place in the veld. He grudgingly follows me. The smell of baked grass lingers in the bitter air. I close my eyes like somebody in deep prayer. I am grateful when it is all over.

As he takes out the money from his coat, something drops into the grass. I receive the money and stutter something about relieving myself. Did he notice that he dropped something? Something in me wants me to tell him that he dropped something but my dry lips are glued together. The tall man hobbles away into the night. His strides are shorter.

My heart pounds with anticipation. I wait for a full minute to make sure that he is gone. My shaky hands grope on the damp grass of the veld. My heart sinks for a moment. It is not a wallet but I can feel its slippery texture under my numb fingers. It is a cellphone! I run away towards the township.

Back home at our shack, my chest is burning but my fingers and lips are stiff and heavy. Gogo opens the door for me and Andile is sleeping soundly on the floor. She tucks herself back into the blankets next to Andile. I place the phone under my pillow and leave for Xoliswa's shack. Her shack, which she shares with her ailing mother, is not far from ours. The squeaky door cracks open and Xoliswa's somnolent mother wobbles out.

"So she is not yet back?" I ask as I hand her the crumpled money.

"Not yet." She shakes her head.

I reassure her as she closes the door, "I am sure she is

on her way. It is almost dawn."

Gogo is snoring heavily. It must be the flu. I finally inspect the cellphone. I cannot believe my luck. It is an elegant touch-screen phone with a screen as long as my palm. I will sell it to the boys later. The phone rings!

I should have removed the SIM card and switched it off. Could it be the owner trying to trace me? The phone's LCD screen blinks incessantly: *Sweet Wife* is calling. I cannot answer it. I just stare at it and it flickers back at me. Before I can figure out how to switch it off, the phone quivers and whirrs and a new message appears. I open it.

"Love I am thinking of you at this hour but sorry you must be sleeping. Can't wait to see you later at the airport. Remember my flight arrives at 9:30am. Love you".

I fumble with the phone and dismantle it. I am tired but I cannot sleep. Gathering a few twigs I head outside and light a fire to warm myself. There are footsteps behind me. The image of the tall sinister man trying to locate me blinds me for an instant. A small hand touches my shoulder.

"Mama you are back! I did not hear you come in." Andile yawns.

I want to tell him to go back to sleep but he comes and sits next to me, feeding the fire with more twigs. I hug him closer as the wind howls, rattling the tin roofs of the shacks. His warm puny palms stick onto my cold back.

The pristine scent of dawn hovers above our township but Xoliswa is not yet back. Somewhere in the dark a police siren moans through the streets. They never come here. Will the tall man come looking for me at the corner of Mabhena and Mpondo Street? I know it will be days before I can go back to our usual corner, to warm myself around the fire, chirping silently, for my life, my child and Gogo.

FRIDAY NIGHT
Chumisa Paquita N

Sindi

Have I really spent all of Summer without you? We have not seen each other since last November ... That time of the year when all the backpackers arrive in Cape Town. It was the same month you found out why your jeans wouldn't fit anymore and you unexpectedly left for home a day after. I hope you and the one growing inside you are happy and well. And I hope you know that even though your silence is hurtful, I still think about you. You also missed my birthday, but whatever, I can no longer be angry with you for trying to be responsible.

It felt more worthwhile for Zizi to be writing a letter to Sindiswa than to be at yet another party. She had recorded a voice reminder on her phone and written in her notebook more than once, reminding herself to think of Sindi. It was three months since they had spoken, or at least since Sindi had communicated with Zizi. Putting pen to paper felt more real and appropriate for this kind of overdue communication. Touching the paper was like getting closer to the relationship they used to have.

As the Maharani incense wafted around her room she momentarily thought of how the smell had become so familiar in just a few weeks. Now she could not sleep without its scent fortifying the thoughts that would lull her to sleep - secretly selling her grandmother's peaches during summer holidays, future travels, photography excursions to remote towns, romanticised erratic relationships. The moonlight came in perfectly through her window; it shone a light on one of the walls, allowing her to see the large map of Africa she had posted up on her wall. On the day she'd brought it home she put small red crosses on the countries she wanted to visit and a more noticeable red heart next to Zimbabwe. "Africa's only liberated country", she would always think to herself.

On nights like this she memorised the cities, small towns and capitals of each country, looked up images of the major cities and made ever-changing lists of the reasons why each country was important to visit. Nigeria; "to learn Yoruba, visit The Shrine,

65

for the music and the ambitious men and to read a Nigerian book in Nigeria". Zimbabwe; "just to see for myself". Cameroon; "for its authentic film industry, the art scene and to meet the people who belong to it". Burkina Faso; "to walk in Sankara's land".

Have you noticed that European and American travellers can be called "tourists, ex-pats, backpackers" and other polite terms while African travellers are plainly labelled as "foreigner", even on our continent? Or maybe we Africans are never just travelling. You and me noticed everything and that's why this city drove us crazy. And yazi tshomi it still drives me crazy.

In the four months that Sindi had been away, Zizi had moved out of her father's house to share an apartment with her friend Khanya. She had become delirious with the idea of freedom. Delirious because just knowing that she can do whatever, whenever, was much more exciting than the actual realisation of this freedom she did not even know how to define. This delirium was caused by living in a space that expanded and contracted as and when she needed it to. Unlike the stuffy, sanitised Northern Suburbs of Cape Town, the city centre was more welcoming of her mistakes and learning.

It hardly ever stifled her questioning, but when it did she thrived on the challenge of deciphering the origins of her thoughts. Thoughts about race and politics that back in the old neighbourhood felt taboo even in her head. The myth of the Rainbow Nation. The myth of equality. The sheer lie of what Cape Town is, or is not. She was in (White) Liberal Land now, some kind of flashy Bohemia where her thoughts were allowed to become spoken words – even if they were too extreme or radical for some of the people who heard them.

Zizi's phone buzzed.

"Do you want to split for a banky?" a text from Khanya. She calculated, *100 bucks for drinks in case we end up going out, fifty bucks for anything extra,* and quickly replied before she thought about it any longer.

"Cool. I've got 50 bucks."

Khanya arrived home with the banky of ganja and a bottle of Pinot Noir, her favourite since she was buying. Zizi rolled three joints, two for now one for later, while Khanya spoke about her day at work. Khanya's job at a glossy women's magazine always provided stories that they could fill moments of silence with. They felt the same way about most women's magazines – over-sexualised, non-journalistic, white-gazey fluff. Khanya hated her job because they never took her input seriously. The editors expected her to speak on behalf of the black market yet when she did they questioned her insight.

On nights like this she memorised the cities, small towns and capitals of each country, looked up images of the major cities and made ever-changing lists of the reasons why each country was important to visit. Nigeria; "to learn Yoruba, visit The Shrine, for the music and the ambitious men and to read a Nigerian book in Nigeria". Zimbabwe; "just to see for myself". Cameroon; "for its authentic film industry, the art scene and to meet the people who belong to it". Burkina Faso; "to walk in Sankara's land".

Have you noticed that European and American travellers can be called "tourists, ex-pats, backpackers" and other polite terms while African travellers are plainly labelled as "foreigner", even on our continent? Or maybe we Africans are never just travelling. You and me noticed everything and that's why this city drove us crazy. And yazi tshomi it still drives me crazy.

In the four months that Sindi had been away, Zizi had moved out of her father's house to share an apartment with her friend Khanya. She had become delirious with the idea of freedom. Delirious because just knowing that she can do whatever, whenever, was much more exciting than the actual realisation of this freedom she did not even know how to define. This delirium was caused by living in a space that expanded and contracted as and when she needed it to. Unlike the stuffy, sanitised Northern Suburbs of Cape Town, the city centre was more welcoming of her mistakes and learning.

It hardly ever stifled her questioning, but when it did she thrived on the challenge of deciphering the origins of her thoughts. Thoughts about race and politics that back in the old neighbourhood felt taboo even in her head. The myth of the Rainbow Nation. The myth of equality. The sheer lie of what Cape Town is, or is not. She was in (White) Liberal Land now, some kind of flashy Bohemia where her thoughts were allowed to become

67

spoken words – even if they were too extreme or radical for some of the people who heard them.

Zizi's phone buzzed.

"Do you want to split for a banky?" a text from Khanya.

She calculated, 100 bucks for drinks in case we end up going out, fifty bucks for anything extra, and quickly replied before she thought about it any longer.

"Cool. I've got 50 bucks."

Khanya arrived home with the banky of ganja and a bottle of Pinot Noir, her favourite since she was buying. Zizi rolled three joints, two for now one for later, while Khanya spoke about her day at work. Khanya's job at a glossy women's magazine always provided stories that they could fill moments of silence with. They felt the same way about most women's magazines – over-sexualised, non-journalistic, white-gazey fluff. Khanya hated her job because they never took her input seriously. The editors expected her to speak on behalf of the black market yet when she did they questioned her insight.

Zizi was brief about her day, mentioning the chicken livers she cooked for lunch and figuring out their faulty kettle. She meant to deter Khanya from asking about the interview she went for in the morning. She had left the over-polished office of a corporate event company still feeling the odd, limp handshake she was offered as a final sign of rejection.

Drinking wine and smoking in the kitchen was always the best part of Zizi's nights. The prelude to new experiences that she would start imagining while they listened to Fela or Phillip Tabane or Outkast or a mix of everything because they disagreed on what should be played next.

So I've been freelancing since you left and now that Summer is over, I'm doing a lot less shoots – which means it's job search time. I'm stuck between self-righteous self-pity for not being where I planned to be at twenty-three and being

totally disgusted with my laziness. On a good morning when I'm high, I might give myself a brief pat on the back and tell myself that one day I'll be the most respected and acclaimed photographer out of this vast continent.

The wine finished and they decided it was time to go out. Zizi put the third joint into her bag and they left the house. They walked silently to their usual spot, Bassment. Khanya was hoping to see her on and off again man Tendai, Zizi was just hoping to experience something enlightening.

Bassment smelled of the Maharani incense Zizi loved so much, wood-floor polish, pure tobacco and good intentions. It was a compact jazz bar that seemed to stretch as much as it needed to, to fit whoever wanted to enter. On big nights when a popular band was playing, the narrow building never seemed to be full enough; it expanded to fit the people and the energies they brought. This place had its own rules and its own unique crowd of painters, writers, musicians, filmmakers, photographers and dancers. Zizi always thought of Bassment's regular crowd as the loose ends of the city, just like herself; people she could complain to, about the absurdity of Cape Town.

Khanya separated from Zizi soon after they entered the building. Tendai had pulled her to the dance floor. Zizi caught the bar lady's eye. Comfort nodded in salutation and raised an empty wine glass, Zizi nodded and smiled. The whole building was vibrating.

It was one of those nights that a movie would depict as a night of a full moon, when everyone transforms and transcends into their true selves in what feels and looks like an underground charismatic church service. A night that would only end after sunrise, after the band had performed an hour over what they were booked for and the DJ had sufficiently tired out his congregants with an electrifying, heavy playlist.

One young woman was in a trance on the dance-floor. Her strapless, vintage dress kept slipping down to reveal her breasts. She wore braids that reached down to her waist. Each time she jumped, the braids covered or exposed her breasts. After the second slip no one even paid her attention. She was part of a sequence of movements and her stomping was only part of the greater piece. Everyone would think about it the next day and remember that it was beautiful and necessary.

Bassment is exactly the way you left it. If not, then it's

probably better. As you might expect I still go there for questionable reasons (sometimes). Questionable in the sense that I would leave my dark room on a still night and carry my wistful mood to the doors of Bassment, just because of the thought of Nyalla. I scold myself Sindi and try to stop myself. But my willpower is low when I haven't felt his gaze for some time.

* * *

Sindi had been there on the night that Nyalla and Zizi met outside the entrance of Bassment. He was in Cape Town from Cameroon for an artist's residency and was considering making his stay more long-term. It was a Tuesday night, one of the calmer nights for the club. Zizi and Sindi were standing outside enjoying fresh air when Nyalla greeted them and walked into the building.

He said, "Good to see you," and gave a brief nod as he respectfully put his right hand to his chest.

By the end of the night they were sitting on a mattress on the floor of his studio, drinking ginger and honey tea. Zizi and Nyalla spent almost everyday of the next three months with each other in Nyalla's studio - talking, painting, taking photographs, and making love. She was the one who caught him burning one of his paintings during a bout of self-doubt, she had helped him come up with the title of his exhibition, and on the night that his exhibition opened, she noticed how much Nyalla revelled in the attention, contrary to the bashful man she knew. If his art were a person, it would have a fist raised to the sky.

Then one afternoon, she found him and a blonde woman on the mattress in his studio, lips locked and heedless.

* * *

Zizi positioned herself on a bar stool in a corner, Comfort timeously placed a glass of their house red in front of her. The spot gave her a good view of the dance floor and the main door. As much as the mood promised memorable images and conversations, Zizi didn't quite feel like she would make it to the end of the night. Not unless Nyalla walked in.

"Hey sister," an American accent broke her gaze from the DJ.

Zizi flinched as if the words were a dirty hand trying to

70

touch her. She took a sip of her wine and looked away. "Excuse me, is this seat taken?" the voice asked. "No."

The woman sat on the stool next to Zizi. She looked at Zizi and grinned.

"Hi, I'm Alexis."

"I'm Zizikazi." They shook hands.

"Wow, I don't know if I'm going to be able to say that!" Alexis said as she giggled.

Zizi took another sip of her wine and waited for the next affliction.

"What do your friends call you?"

"Zizikazi."

"It's a really pretty name, though." Alexis bit her lip nervously then smiled before ordering a local beer.

Marvin Gaye's 'Got To Give It Up' came on, DJ Sello nodded and smiled coyly to himself as his congregants extolled him. Fist-bumps reigned as some people came on to the small stage to thank him personally for the blessings. Surrounded by crates of vinyls, his turntables and the laudation, it was not clear whether he was on a pulpit or a throne. Khanya caught Zizi's gaze and called her to the dance floor. Zizi shook her head and Khanya rejoined the rhythm of movements.

"Oh my God, I love your hair," said Alexis.

Before Zizi had time to respond, Alexis had already run her fingers through her hair. Zizi backed her head away and ran her own hand through her Afro as if to check if it was all still there.

"What makes you think you can do that?" Zizi asked.

"I'm sorry, I just wanted to feel it."

"Don't you think you should ask me before you touch me?"

"I'm sorry sister, I just wanted to know how it feels." "You didn't make an effort to say my name, you touch my hair without asking and then you call me 'sister'?"

"I'm just trying to get into your culture. I'm sorry."

Khanya came to stand next to Zizi, her face gleaming with sweat. Her smile slowly faded as she caught on that this was not a jovial conversation.

"You can't just get into my culture. Especially not by

touching my hair and calling me sister," Zizi said.

"Come upstairs with me," Khanya said, "light one up."

Zizi stood up and took her half-empty glass of wine, leaving Alexis without saying a word or giving her a look. Khanya held Zizi's hand as they walked up the narrow staircase of Bassment. The upstairs was lit up. Bassment regulars called it The Purple Room. It was painted a dark purple and had mismatched sofas and cushions on the floor. A mural of Sathima Bea Benjamin, her face brooding and shadowed, adorned the wall opposite the stairs. Unlike downstairs, the distinctive smell was not only of incense but also the smoke from different strains of ganja. The space was lively yet easy going. Small groups occupied different parts of the room; either deep in conversation, smoking, or both. Zizi and Khanya joined a group, greeted everyone and were soon assimilated into the pace of the room.

Coming to Bassment, Zizi's mood was already leaden, but the encounter with Alexis weighed her down further. Her sense of autonomy was stolen. Of all the clubs or bars in Cape Town, this was where she was accountable to no one but herself. The experience with Alexis was atypical for Bassment, an aggravating reminder that maybe autonomy didn't really exist for the black person in Cape Town.

"I'm trying not to be mad so don't bring it up," Zizi whispered into Khanya's ear.

"What happened?" "The usual, my name." Khanya waited.

"Only this time I was called sister. And she touched my hair without asking."

"Damn. Well, let's smoke and forget about her."

Zizi settled against the wall with her almost empty glass of wine still in her hand. The Purple Room didn't need many people to make it seem full. She felt a serene daze creep up on her as she looked around the room, at the people laughing genuinely and being light about life.

Sindi, this city is too hostile to experience alone. I feel like it forces people to behave in ugly, unnatural ways. Large monuments of men we don't know tower over us and remind me every day that this city does not belong to us. I can just imagine you say, "My friend you can do whatever you want". Can I really? Maybe I can do whatever I want but can I say whatever I want? Can I think whatever I want to think? I don't know, I'm trying. The only thing I can rely on is a good high. When it gets too complicated I can smoke and feel my mind clear. I start to think of beautiful things like streets void of election banners, trains with no class partitions and a glorious heap of ash – the remains of that stupid statue of a Dutch coloniser that I must walk past every day on my way home.

"Zizi I'm going back downstairs to Tendai. Are you coming?" asked Khanya.

"I think I'll just get a cab home. I'll see you in the morning?"

Khanya nodded and smiled. They would probably see each other late afternoon the next day, when Khanya came back from Tendai's place.

Khanya walked Zizi out of Bassment.

It was still crazy and crowded in the street, the clubs and bars were still a few hours away from closing and the police vans were just starting to become visible.

"There's your man," Khanya said, looking across the street to a man who was standing alone smoking a cigarette.

Zizi turned and smiled at him, her heart knocking on her better judgement and her armpits tingling as she willed him to notice her.

"Do you think I should go say 'hi'?" Zizi asked.

Khanya stayed silent.

"He didn't tell you he was back in the country," Khanya said.

Zizi felt Khanya's eyes on her while she watched Nyalla. The real figure of him and not the lookalikes she had trained herself to ignore.

Zizi looked at Khanya. "I'm going to go say 'hi'."

Khanya stayed silent.

A woman coming from lower down the street approached him. Nyalla put out his cigarette and watched the beaming woman until she was standing right in front of him. He might have smiled back. They shared a long hug; his hand was on her lower back, pulling her against him. Then she kissed him, the blonde woman. Up until the kiss, Zizi believed that the woman might simply ask for a lighter or where she could find a cab.

Khanya held Zizi's hand and rubbed gently with her thumb; she pulled her up towards the corner of the street where the cabs always idled. Zizi stopped at the first cab she saw and got inside.

"That was the worst," Zizi said. "I'll see you tomorrow."

"Call me when you get home." "Okay."

Zizi left with the cab driver.

Anyway I'm trying to grow up you know? Trying to become my real self, whoever that is - without you, without the high walls of my father's home, without Nyalla and his blondes. I know you're doing the same where you are and I'll see you when I see you.

I miss you always, Zizikazi.

INSIDE-OUTSIDE
Nyachiro L Kasese

My addictions often look like my mother. I am three years old and they are holding me away from her. They are saying my weak eyes will be the reason my father won't make it back. I am five and in my dreams my father is running. Away. Almost as if something in my direction is chasing him. I am seven and my father comes to steal me away. I am a confusion growing like a cancer in the head inside my head. My mother is a sorrowful flower garden full of gardenias no one is allowed to pick. We are a montage of otherness. My sister is a dozen prayers knitted together from the gardenias inside my mother's head. She is the reason our pastor won't let us into church anymore. She is the reason our prayers are stuck to the ceiling.

It is 1998, and minding our own business is what my sister and I do best. We are hopscotch, hide-and-seek kids. We are adventurous, searching, finding. We are storytellers, composers, writers and dreamers. We are five and twelve years of age and my golden bush of curls runs all the way down my spine and sometimes I am called *muzungu*. I have come to love this alienating name. I have come to associate it with betterness. Otherness.

My father despises it. He says it gives him nightmares he would not talk about in the brightest of lights. We believe him. There are some things that happen in the darkness of our house in spaces that no light is ever supposed to enter. There was a secret once that lurked in the floorboards of our house. On my fifteenth birthday it grew wings and flew out of my parent's room with such violence that there was an earthquake within our minds and a tremor within the palms of our hands.

Once upon a time, I am unborn. Uncreated. And my mother has not conceived. She is married two years and the in-laws are talking. They are demanding their *mahari* back because they were sold "damaged" goods. My mother works as the personal assistant to the white man living at the bottom of their street. Mr Aspen they called him. My father is the man people refer to as teacher. I have never known him to teach. But he is a learning man.

My mother is not a small woman, she is a mountain that moves things. On other days she is a volcano. Erupting. Setting things and people on fire without meaning to. My grandmother says that's what happened that night at Mr Aspen's house. She says my mother set Mr Aspen on fire and he forced his fire inside her until it turned to ashes and there was me. I was fifteen when I found this out. I knew nothing of forest fires then, knew nothing of how they could burn through whole generations of families. My father went looking for my mother that night. He found her sitting in the dark street, her face an army of fallen soldiers who even years after I was born had not risen.

I am five years old and my father is leaving. He does not know how to communicate with fallen soldiers. For four years he was trying to build victory into their spinal chords, attempting to bring life back to them. When I was born my father, knowing I was not his own, held me to his heart knowing I came from his own and therefore I was his regardless of how I came to be within her. He did all he could to make a queen of her, to rid her of the rags and dirt she thought she wore. I am five years old and my father has given up turning paupers and beggars into queens. He walks away in the night and my mother holds me away from her saying my weak eyes will be the reason he will not come back.

My father has been back for seven years. He is now a learning man. We are fourteen and seven years old. There is a knock on our living room door. My father's shame stands in our doorway in the form of a ten-year-old boy. I am told he is my brother. This news is fed to us like leftovers thrown out to the dogs. We take no offence and receive this news with as much grace as one can muster at the age of fourteen without breaking into tears. We have lived long enough to know when to not ask questions, when to disappear in a room full of awkwardness and potential death from falling secrets.

My mother is unaccustomed to falling secrets. Gravity possesses her and her body is a limp noodle. My father is a storm of fear and worry. My grandmother is the avalanche that started it. She is seventy-five and will not die without a son to carry her husband's name. She is a detective that finds what she is looking

76

for even if it may not exist. She is a wolf that locates the scent of her family's seed in the city my father inhabited when he left us. She is the tidal wave that pours this awkward boy into our living room at an ungodly hour.

The boy that is my brother is a vessel of strangeness. Otherness maybe. We tiptoe around him for the next few days as he tiptoes around my mother, aware of the heaviness he has become in the semi-lightness of our house. He is given a name that means "bastard" by the neighbours. He likes that he has his own room, with his own bed. He likes that our bathroom contains a toilet that is not a hole in the ground. We know this because we see the look on his face. Also, he tells this to my younger sister. They have become friends. I conclude that he is the child of a woman with breast milk for ammunition and a welcoming vagina for armour. A struggling but perhaps a surviving woman.

A great man dies and my grandmother sits in the ashes of our second kitchen as she attempts to explain his greatness without breaking. The brother who wasn't my brother until a few months ago points out that greatness needs no explaining. Somehow he dares to have a voice in a place that is still shifting and making room for his accommodation. He dares to assume the position of someone whose opinion, let alone whose existence, matters.

My seven-year-old sister punches him in the stomach and tells him to be quiet. At her age she understands the holiness that outlines story telling, great or small. She sits by the ashes with our grandmother, comfortable enough with discomfort, she will be the one to later narrate this story to her dolls and cats as she plays school with them.

My brother who is now referred to as my brother is friends with boys who sell little gods that come in sachets you can buy from someone who knows someone. I know this because I have seen them in the midst of their "temple" at the back of the schoolyard bent over in a tight circle as if in prayer. I should report this temple to my parents. I should tell them of the incense burnt there and the lack of godliness in my brother's eyes as he attempts to make his way home.

But I do not say anything to my parents. He is a boy

embodying intelligence. He is an aspiring mathematician. He is nice to my sister. Also, I am old enough to understand the dull ache that comes from being the one brick in the wall that does not fit right. I understand the need to be rebellious. The hunger for importance.

My sister walks home one day like falling crescendos. The music in her voice box is at an octave so low only my mother can hear. She holds her close to her chest and lets her body move to the sound of music only she can hear. I accidentally walk in on this dance and I immediately know a war has started at the meeting of my sister's legs. Eleven months later my sister evolves into a poem I find underneath her pillow and confuse for a suicide note:

> There are no pictures on the walls of our living room. My
> father says they look like bloodstains on our white
> walls and sins should never be put on display like that.
> And so my brother isn't really my brother.
> He is a photo that we put down so the neighbours would
> not feel embarrassed when they come to borrow some sugar.
> He is a full stop to a sentence no one has the courage to
> finish,
> so it just hangs there.
> My mother is a praying woman who understands that
> her eldest son is a preying man,
> so she knows God will understand if she chooses to omit
> his name over prayers,
> or if she chooses to kill him in conversations with the
> neighbourhood women.
> I wear his shame like a loosely-fitting maternity dress,
> like abortions have been chasing me all my life.
> And I have nothing but pictures of pregnancies that I
> cannot hang on walls to prove this.
> And my youngest brother isn't really my brother,
> he looks like my father,
> but so does my older brother.

I have known people to kill themselves over a bar of

soap. I have known people to kill themselves with a bar of soap. The man nextdoor attempts to fix leaking water pipes with his adulterous wife's bra straps. The man next door to the man next door walks out to find the bra straps he once bought his mistress being tied to leaking water pipes. He confuses them for her tears. This is the randomness that is my mind.

My brother does not come home that night. Or the night after. He shows up two weeks later looking like one of the thieves on either side of the lord's cross. He was away long enough for my mother to piece two and two together in order to get betrayal. She knows a thing or two about Maths, my mother.

My grandmother was the wind that shook the family tree that dropped my brother. Her need for a grandson has made a battlefield of our house. She walks along the shadows of our house at night and fakes illness that requires her to be asleep or alone in her room in the daytime. My father starts searching for gods that would explain life to him. I do not know if he actually ever found them. I doubt he ever did.

* * *

Yesterday the phone rings at three in the morning and I am in a dream where it is three o'clock and it is the devil's hour and he is telling me of how my brother just died. I am awake and I am attempting life. I am attempting movement and questions. I am asking questions I know answers to, like "what do you mean *my* brother? *Which* brother?"

I attempt lighting a cigarette to calm the tremor within my fingers. I am failing. And I now understand how earthquakes can deactivate whole bodies of land. I am calling airlines to book the earliest possible flight back home. I am on a flight home.

I am home and my brother is not there to receive me. My sister is here instead. She appears to be a rock in a land where everything is sand or liquid or fluid. She hugs me tightly and I hold on maybe a second too long before I let go and throw my bags in the back of her car. No words have been said between us in the time it takes for me to appear at the airport and disappear into her car. I believe there are none. Until she parks at the side of the road and faces me.

"Dad killed Twazi. It was an accident. He was sneaking

back into the house late at night and dad thought he was a thief. Did they tell you how he died?"

"No. I did not ask. How did he die?"

"It was a panga. He was jumping in through the windows at the back. I figure he was out hanging with those sinful men at their temple. The alarm went off as soon as his head was in. When dad got there he only saw a head and a body attempting to make its way into our house. So he took a panga and cut the head off. I didn't even know we had a panga. But you know these house robbery things. They robbed us a couple of months ago. They scared the living daylights out of ma. Papa thought it was them coming back again."

She does not wait for me to respond. She starts the car and we are driving through once familiar roads and streets and houses. I am silence at this point. I am nothing that can make a sound. I am calculating, finding averages and percentages on the chances of my sister being wrong. I am a mathematician after all. I believe in the validity of numbers when it comes to the assessing of a situation.

In my parents' house there is strangeness on top of the strangers and gossip searchers disguised in the clothes of mourners. The media holds no respect for our family as they try to sell tabloids of the man that mistakes *his own flesh and blood for a thief* and the radio anchor on the evening show wonders, "is it not our flesh and blood that steal from us?" And I turn off the radio and focus on the mourners that are mourning for a man they never knew.

I stumble upon an argument amongst the relatives. The question of where to bury Twazi's body is somehow contingent on whether he died inside or outside the house. My father's eldest brother argues that his head fell into the house and the head is the source of all functions therefore he died inside. My father's second eldest brother counter argues with *"the heart is more important"*, so he died outside because that is where his body fell. My father's silence is an argument he is having on his own.

"Inside-Outside. That is where he died. Inside-outside." I say and evacuate the room.

I have dared to have a voice in the presence of men. I

have dared to have an opinion. The silence that is their voices, or shock, follows me as I make my way to our little orchard at the back of the house to have a cigarette and maybe some peace of mind. Some numbers. Some calculations. Just anything solid and unchanging that I can rely on and hold on to.

The family pastor requires a member of the family to say a word or two before the burial. My grandmother surprises everyone including herself by hobbling up to the front of the room. Her voice box has been missing for years and we sit up in our seats anticipating the mimic of a mime. She turns to face the rest of the room and says, *"There is something about hope that resembles a game of Russian roulette"* before she breaks into song.

* * *

We are sitting in my kitchen the night before your wedding. We're a happy mess filled with wine and dreaming of the future you are going to have with a man no one understands why you love. Maybe you have had one too many. Maybe I have too. But it doesn't matter.

You say to me, *"Remember the night Twazi died?"*

Of course I remember. No one forgets. But I do not say this to you. I nod my head instead.

You say. *"Well, it was me. It wasn't dad who killed him. It was me. It wasn't an accident either. I hadn't planned it. But I saw the opportunity and I took it."*

KAWESA
Arnold N Musalia

There had always been that little house two compounds away from my home, across the street from Jimi Ngwazi's home. At least it has been there as long as most of us could remember … 'Us' meaning the group of six boys who always hung out together – and just about everyone else from Jilona village. You wouldn't know Jilona because it is not even on the map of Kenya. Just a tiny village nestled in the palm of Busomba County.

Kawesa and her grandmother had not always lived in Jilona. And come to think of it, neither she nor the old woman she lived with had ever told anyone that they were related. It was just assumed so by everyone. People jump to conclusions from what they observe and proceed to force their assumptions to be the truth. Afterwards, no one even remembered why they had all called her 'Kawesa' … It turned out at the very end that no one had ever actually asked her what her name was … And she had never really introduced herself to anyone. But *this* is the beginning.

I remember quite clearly when Kawesa and the old woman came to Jilona. It was around about the time there had been very heavy rains and everyone had been so worried that there may not be any harvest that season if the rains persisted. The big people in Nairobi said over the radio that the rains were called 'elonino', and they will be happening for a long time yet. It was Jimi Ngwazi's mother who came and told my mother that new people had moved into the little abandoned house across the road from her place.

"What kind of people?" Mami had asked her, leaning across the table, all the better to hear Jimi Ngwazi's mother. The visitor clutched the mug of hot tea with both hands to try and drive some of the chill from her body.

"I saw a young girl … Like my Silwa … She had the windows open and there was a pair of shoes outside the door …" Silwa was Jim Ngwazi's elder sister.

"Is a child that age going to stay alone in the house?" Mami wondered loudly.

"I don't think so … That's why I said there must be other

people beside her."

I was amused that Jimi Ngwazi's mother had not just gone straight to meet her new neighbours ... Why had she instead come all the way to speculate with my mother? Perhaps it was just because it was more exciting for her that way. Suspense and a sort of thrill from wondering and speculating exactly who and how the new neighbours would turn out to be. Were they rich? Okay ...Hardly likely ... Or were they poor enough to be a bother, borrowing things every now and then and not having anything to give in return? Were they the type that minded their business and kept themselves to themselves or would they be picking quarrels every time the chickens scratched about in their yard or if they thought the volume of your radio was turned on too loud? As the two women continued sharing their worries, fears and hopes about the new neighbours, I quietly sneaked out of the house to go and see for myself.

The rain had fizzled down from the furious downpour that had raged for most of the previous night, to the steady, determined drizzle that had stubbornly sprinkled the earth with an arduous determination ... Now all they had left behind to carry on their presence was a grey mist that hung gloomily all over or drifted around slowly on the wings of the occasional breeze.

The girl Jimi Ngwazi's mother had talked about now had the door of the small house open and was sweeping around the doorway with a broom made from stiff grasses. She was slim and light-complexioned, *that* I could see from the road as I slowly strolled past, looking at her from the corner of my eye , so that she wouldn't catch me staring. And she was around Silwa's age too, seventeen ... Only Silwa was short and black with cheeks like the bellies of two tea kettles hinged together by a loose-lipped mouth, her stubby chin trying desperately to hide underneath. *This* girl was quite pretty.

She paused in her sweeping and humming of a little tune and actually smiled at me. She had shallow dimples, not in the middle where normal dimples usually go, but up higher, closer to the nose, which made them even more mesmerizing. I passed real close to the house because I wanted to see as much as I could before I crossed over to Jimi Ngwazi's. She had long hair done up in four braids that dangled on her shoulders.

I thought then that she might not be of our people. Women from Jilona were mostly shorter with darker skins and hardly any dimples at all.

"Have you seen her?" Jim Ngwazi asked as soon as I got to his house. I had never seen him so excited. He was fourteen, just like me and the others in our group, except for Toma who was sixteen. All of us had started getting excited about girls and how they looked and such stuff. And Kawesa, as people started calling her, caused quite some excitement among the boys in Jilona. She was a welcome distraction from the elonino that kept steadily on for quite a few weeks more. She spoke our language with a noticeable accent, but we understood her. It turned out that she had moved into the previously deserted house with an older woman, whom we all decided was her grandmother. Everyone just started calling her 'koko' – Grandmother. Why! We never really thought it strange that Kawesa and Koko were never seen at the same time. Kawesa was mostly seen in the mornings up to around midday, usually hawking samosas around the village.

Koko came out in the evenings, tottering around with the aid of a stout walking staff. She didn't seem 'all there', if you ask me ... And everyone seemed to think so, although of course one doesn't talk about such things. All people are God's people and old people deserve respect. She was a chirpy old soul, who cheerfully greeted everyone she met and started a conversation with anyone willing to stop and listen. Only that no one ever took the things she said seriously, because they never made any sense.

"A big fat one I had yesterday," she would say sometimes, "it will last me quite a while ... A big fat delicious one!" She would wink mischievously, while chuckling and sucking on her toothless gums. Sometimes it would be, "a skinny one, all bones ... But what could I do ... That's all there was ... It will make do *he he he* ... not much meat on the bones," she would cheerfully inform whoever cared to listen. Most people tried to humour her as much as possible, and pretended they understood whatever she was saying quite perfectly. And after a few weeks, children would call out to her and ask whether she had 'killed a fat one or a thin one'. The physical condition of her supposed kill was the only topic she ever discussed, even with the grownups.

One thing that was unanimously agreed on by the people of Jilona was that the samosas that Kawesa hawked were the best anyone had ever tasted. They had a flavour that no one could quite make out. The assumption was that when Kawesa disappeared mysteriously in the afternoons and evenings, she went to find and buy the meat and mysterious ingredients she put in the small pies. She never told anyone that, we all just 'used common sense' and came to that conclusion. In the mornings, the aroma of cooking samosas would drift alluringly from the little house across the road from Jimi Ngwazi's and people would troop over to buy some for their breakfast or to pack for lunch.

You could never get enough of Kawesa's samosas. Not ever! Koko slept through the time her granddaughter cooked and sold samosas...the whole day, but then she was old. Old people needed their rest. Everyone knew that, so no one ever asked where Koko was when she could not be seen. None of the women of Jilona were ever able to wiggle out Kawesa's secret samosa recipe. Not even Jimi Ngwazi's mother, about whom was said a secret could never be hidden.

Around the time that Kawesa and her grandmother mysteriously appeared in Jilona, there had been numerous reports in the local press about the disappearance of children in Butengo and Kyalangwa villages some distance away from Jilona. Those who listened at all had heard about it over the radio. There had been reports in the newspapers too perhaps, but no one had the money to waste on those, except perhaps Mwalimu Handa, the headmaster of the local school. Chief Kilule, who was our village headman, had mentioned it in passing in a baraza he had called to discuss land issues and other more important matters.

The children who had disappeared belonged to other people from other villages. When things happen to people we don't know, they could as well have happened on the moon. Even if the people involved came from a village just a few miles away. No one really paid much attention to the stories ... Perhaps the village housewives did, when they had nothing more interesting to discuss.

When the children of the village were sent to Kawesa's

little house to buy samosas in the morning, she always entertained them with stories ... Folk stories more interesting than any other that the children had ever been told by their parents or grandparents. Stories about wily little hares that tricked wolves and hyenas and other fierce animals. Stories about people who did all sorts of intriguing and funny things that left the children howling with laughter.

One day she told the tale of a girl who, newly married and too shy to ask for some food when she was starving, tried to steal a piece of hot meat from her grandmother's pot. Then she was caught and had to pretend that she had suddenly caught mumps. There was something about the way Kawesa spun her tales. She became the characters in the stories when she told them, her cheeks puffing up with the piece of stolen meat and her face twisting with agony as the bride's cheeks were burned with a hot coal, to cure her fake mumps, till she spat out the stolen meat.

And so as the days went by. The elonino was over and the sun started rising at the expected time, warming the land with her radiant smile and slowly resurrecting the seeds that had been buried into the ground that would rise as plants, taller and lusher, defying the big people on the radio who had predicted a famine.

Then Jimi Ngwazi got lost. Just like that! Okay, of course he was not a needle that fell to the floor and somehow disappeared or a coin that someone dropped somewhere on the road on the way to the shop. Jimi Ngwazi was a living, breathing human being aged fourteen years old. He had been at school from morning to four o'clock. Then he had left with the other children ... With us! Bowa, Chigutya, Gomwe, Eriya and I, Tuwayi, the six of us who were together most of the time. Later, he had gone to Mayi Fumbwa's place to fetch the milk, something he always did in the evenings. But that was the last evening he would leave home on that particular errand.

After his mother had waited long enough, she looked for a nice strong cypress cane and set off to the street corner where she was sure she would find Jimi Ngwazi shooting marbles with the rest of our group. But he wasn't there! And neither was he to be found at Mayi Fumbwa's place. He had collected the milk and left hours ago. After it had been established that Jimi Ngwazi was not in any of the homes in Jilona, the alarm was raised and Chief Kilule and his men – with most of the able villagers volunteering to help – literally turned the entire village upside down; searched every bush, well, stream and just about every possible place that a fourteen year old boy could hide...or his body hidden if it came to that.

After all that could be done had been done and the police at Busomba Police Post duly informed, everyone kind of assumed that Jimi Ngwazi was gone to some place from which there could be no return. The women took turns sitting with his mother and the men walked around with long, dark faces. Us children were warned to never go about alone and to avoid being outside after dark.

One thing that didn't seem affected by the dark turn of events was Koko, Kawesa and her samosas. The day right after Jimi Ngwazi disappeared, we all went to her house for the delicious treats as usual. And in the evening Koko came out of the hut and tottered along the road that led to Kiyonga, chuckling with what seemed like more satisfaction and joy than usual at the plumpness and juiciness of her catch the previous day. Everyone, despite the sombre mood, indulged her by sharing her excitement about the physical condition of her supposed catch.

Two days later, neither Jimi Ngwazi, nor anything that could lead to the unravelling of the mystery of his disappearance had been found. Not even one scrap of the shirt he had worn! Just like the children from the far off villages that we had heard about, he had disappeared without trace. It was around then that Kawesa told us the story about the Mangidi, a mysterious spirit creature. When I look back, she seemed to take a ghoulish pleasure in telling this story.

"The Mangidi was there, before the first man was born," she told the small group of children squatting and standing around her charcoal brazier as she deftly turned the samosas in her deep bellied pan. "It sustains itself by drawing life blood from young humans. From the beginning of time, it has walked this earth, moving from one place to another, taking various forms, either human or animal. But whatever form it takes, it has to be new by day and older as the day grows old. If it takes the form of a handsome young warrior," she fluttered her eyebrows a little, "as the evening draws near, it will slowly turn into a toothless wizened old geezer," she crunched her face and sucked her lips in to imitate a caved in, toothless mouth of an old man and all the children squealed with laughter.

"If it changes itself into a nice fat cow with swollen udders during the day, in the evening it will be a wizened cow with a scabby skin with its ribs showing through ..." As Kawesa continued making the other kids laugh with her tale about the Mangidi, a chilly wind congealed the very marrow in my bones. Something about Kawesa's story made me uneasy.

Later that evening Mami sent me over to Ma Shungwi's home to borrow the flat pan for making chapatti. Ma Shungwi lived just a few metres away from our home, I could dash over and be back within a minute.

I had collected the pan and was making my way around the little bush at the back of Ma Shungwi's place when I suddenly felt someone firmly grasp my right hand. I turned around and looked into Koko's face ... Kawesa's? I had never had the chance to look at Koko close up. She always had this headscarf covering most of her face. Now I could clearly see that Koko was just a very old Kawesa!

She had a sharp, awl-like piece of metal lifted high in her right hand. There was none of Kawesa's pretty dimples and jovialness nor Koko's twinkling eyes in the face I saw. Just something cold, cruel and not human at all! Zobby, Ma Shungwi's puppy gave a loud yelp and started barking furiously, waking me from my fear induced trance. I owe my life to that dog though I will never know how I made it back to Mami's kitchen. It was more *my* screams than Mami's that roused the entire village.

Twelve years later, I still have the scars, one an inch or so longer than the other, proof when I tell and retell the story of how I – Tuwayi Jumwa – narrowly escaped from the Mangidi. But to date, not even I dare to talk about Kawesa's samosas and the fact that at some point, they may have contained poor Jimi Ngwazi's flesh.

MY BREASTS
Nkiacha Atemnkeng

Two days after I returned to the village from Limbe, where I lived with my older sister Violet, mother sat me down and asked if I had seen my first flower. I was amazed.

"Mother, I see flowers every day," I answered and she laughed.

"Abigail, I don't mean normal flowers. Okay, there is a palm-tree, which has fallen inside you. Very soon palm wine will trickle out of it and form a little puddle. It will be red wine not white. Don't get scared the day it happens okay?"

"Yes, mother," I answered.

"It is normal and simply means you have become a woman."

Why was she talking in a roundabout way? Was she referring to my first menses? I knew something about it from school.

"Just like the palm tree, you will produce red palm wine every month. Something special inside your tree taps the red wine. That's your hibiscus flower. But if you let honeybees lick the entrance where your red wine flows out, then it will stop flowing. So don't let any honeybees lick you until it's time. Do you hear me?"

"Mother, I don't understand."

"I said don't let any honeybee lick the tip of your tree or else you will become pregnant," she said, raising her voice slightly.

I nodded. Did she mean I shouldn't have sex? Was it the taboo word she was avoiding?

"Say yes mother, it's disrespectful to nod at me."

"Yes, mother."

"Abi, you are glowing too like a hibiscus flower. You shouldn't let honey bees suck your nectar before you produce fruit."

"Yes, mother."

"And when your red palm wine flows for the first time, there is something you must do. It's what all the girls in our village

89

do. Is that clear?"

"Yes, mother," I answered even though I was confused, curious about periods and what it meant for girls in the village.

I'm a thirteen-year-old who is spending the long holiday in the village of Letia. I have budding breasts, hips and curves that are attracting the attention of the boys in my village. I admire myself, wondering, "How do I look? Am I beautiful?" I examine my buttocks in the mirror, my thighs and especially my breasts, as they slowly grow into firm pawpaws with pointy nipples sprouting like flower buds.

I started using make up to improve my looks and boys run after me trying to coax me with their numerous I-love-you stories. However, I remember Mother's warning and resist them. Well, all of them except Jimmy. No matter how hard I try, I can't. He is so irresistible with his tall frame, handsome face, hoarse voice and caring nature.

We have been seeing each other almost every day. It started the day he chased me around the trees and accused me of stealing his pineapples. When I insisted that I hadn't, he smiled and told me I had stolen something bigger than his fruits.

"What?"

"Abi, you've stolen my heart."

I melted. When he fondled me the first time, I enjoyed the sensation of his soft warm hands. After we ended our dalliance for the day and he told me he was going home, I went to see him off. When I was about to return, he came to see me off. We saw each other off, back and forth, delirious with joy. I didn't want to let him go. I wanted to be by his side.

One day, we were sitting under the shade of a Kola-nut tree when he said,

"Do you know we've never kissed?"

I replied shyly, "I don't know how to do it. Do you?"

He nodded, staring into my eyes.

The wind halted and the air was still. I could hear the sound of feathers falling to the ground. My heart stopped beating completely when his face moved towards mine. I was nervous and pushed my face forward expecting my lips to meet his. Instead, our noses collided.

He was the first to hold his. "Aii, you hit my nose. You are supposed to tilt your head and open your mouth slightly. That's what you do when you are about to kiss."

"Ah, sorry! I didn't know." I touched my own nose then. It hurt a little.

Jimmy pushed me to the ground and gently planted kisses all over my face. He told me to stay still and lowered his head, tilted his face and brought it towards mine. The tree overhead seemed to grow in size and I opened my mouth slowly. I caught his red lips and sucked them like lollipops, relishing the slippery sounds. His hands were all over my body, probing, stroking and caressing. I could feel the wetness in my pants already and his hard penis, up like a flagpole.

I gawked into his eyes and he whispered, "It tastes like orange juice."

I laughed out loud.

He closed my mouth quickly. "Shh, somebody might hear us."

I removed his hand from my mouth and slapped him playfully. "You fool. How can a kiss taste like orange juice?"

"But your mouth tastes like an orange!" He insisted and made some throaty sounds while unbuttoning my blouse and taking it off. He found my nipples with his fingers and began rubbing them in slow circular sweeps.

I moaned and moaned and suddenly heard him say, "Abi, let's have sex!"

I cringed immediately. "Eem, no, no, I can't! My mother ..."

"Ahh!" He snarled and launched his mouth towards my right breast, sucking my nipple and then proceeding to the left. It felt celestial.

Suddenly, twigs snapped and something shot out of the bushes. We stopped our lovemaking and looked up in fright. I quickly found my blouse and put it back on. It was the slovenly figure of Papa Yallo the hunter, carrying his rifle and staring at us in bemusement. We were rooted to the spot and I felt a pang of shame.

"Look at these idiots!" he said. "When I heard sounds

around here I thought it was a wild bird, only to arrive and see two tiny dogs having sex."

"We were not having…"

"Shut up. Abigail! At your age you *already know a man! What a shame. And you Jimmy.* What is your mouth doing on a woman's breast? Uh? Have you suddenly become a baby sucking a woman's breasts for milk? Wonders shall never end! Leave this place before I shoot you with my gun, he-goat."

Jimmy rose and left quickly, communicating with me through eye contact. I tried to budge but Papa Yallo entrenched me to the spot with his pointing fingers. When he was sure that Jimmy had gone, he turned to me. "*You*, follow me."

My heart was pounding like a jackhammer. We went straight to my house, where Papa Yallo narrated what he'd seen in a torrent of words. Mother flung me to the floor and whipped me until I had cane imprints all over my arms. I cried for the rest of that day. When I had calmed down, I started feeling some abdominal pain, almost like contractions.

The next morning, I realized that I had stained the bed sheet with blood. It was a small red patch. I had just menstruated! Or in mother's metaphorical language, I had just seen my first flower! I laughed. So this was the red palm wine mother was talking about! I examined the small red stain then smelled it.

I heard approaching footsteps and took off the bed sheet quickly, dumping it in a corner. I thought it was Hughes, my brother but it turned out to be mother. When our eyes met, I looked away still fuming about the thrashing.

She stared. "Abigail, why did you take off your bed sheet, is it dirty?"

"No."

"Haven't I told you not to answer me like that when I speak to you? Uh? Naughty child."

"I just bled, that's why I took it off."

"Oh!" the news seemed to silence her a little and she calmed down. Her countenance suddenly went tender. She sat next to me.

"My child, that's your first flower …"

"Mother I know," I cut in.

92

"From now on you need to put on a pad which will stop the bleeds. It means you are now capable of bearing the fruit of the womb. And I *don't* want you pregnant at this age. So you *must* stop this thing you are doing with that foolish boy or else he will get you pregnant or infected with disease and if he does, I will skin you alive, do you hear me?" she barked, pointing her index finger to my skull.

"I didn't do anything with him," I said slowly, "and he's not foolish."

"What was he doing on top of your body? *Uh*? What was his mouth doing on your breast?"

"He didn't sleep with me ..."

"Then *what* did he do?"

I remained silent.

"I should never catch you near him again. You want to bring disgrace upon my head? Children of today! *I* did not know a man until the day I married your father, my dear departed husband. But nowadays, at fourteen you are already opening your legs and letting boys suck your breasts."

The statement stung me like a bee. I had not slept with Jimmy, but I was still mortified.

Mother continued. "Which reminds me. Tomorrow, I will take you to Mama Ajoache."

"What for, Mother?"

She pushed her face towards mine, "if you *must* know, so that she can iron your breasts and stop them growing bigger, so that you won't attract nanny goats to suckle your breasts as though they are drinking milk. They will grow only when you mature and get ripe for marriage."

I shook my head.

"Dare you disrespect that? It is our tradition and you know very well that *every* girl in this village goes through that rite when they start seeing their flower. I know Violet told you." She scowled.

My sister, Violet *had* mentioned breast ironing a couple of times. I knew it was a practice all the girls in our village went through, to prevent their breasts from growing rapidly. So they will not become sexual objects in the eyes of men. So that they will not attract men like muddy ditches attract mosquito larvae. She said the practice helped maintain virginity until marriage.

She also said ironed breasts do not grow very big and she always regretted it because it had impeded her breasts from developing properly. I was always taken aback by the size and nature of Violet's breasts. They looked too small to me and the left one was slightly larger than the right one. She told me once that the deformity developed because her breasts were ironed.

I did not want the same thing to happen to me – having disproportionate breasts all in the name of ancient tradition - even though I had never told sister Violet that. It didn't make much sense to me. The ironing of my breasts will not guarantee that men will not pursue me. It will not stop me from having sex with Jimmy if I want to. And it's nobody's business to whom I lose my virginity, not even my mother's.

My mother stood up suddenly and left the room, then returned moments later and hurled a packet of Faytex pads at me. "Use those. Tomorrow, we'll go to Mama Ajoache's place. She's our village's best breast ironer." Then before leaving, she added, "if you feel any pain or cramps, just lie down and rest. That one has no cure but it won't kill you."

Mama Ajoache's face looked like that of an old statue. She took us to a kitchen and made us sit on bamboo stools. She lit a fire, blowing air into it with her mouth until it caught flame. She put two pepper stone shaped rocks into the fire, letting them absorb heat, maintaining a conversation with my mother about the rotting state of society. About how babies were now sleeping with men and giving birth to babies themselves. In their day, that was unheard of.

I wasn't listening to their conversation. I was dreading the moment when she would use the hot stones to press down my breasts. She examined the stones and my heart sank but she turned back to my mother and they kept talking. Eventually, she turned to me and ordered me to take off my blouse.

My heart skipped to the rafters as I looked at mother. Her eyes ordered me to comply. I took off my blouse slowly. It felt awkward being bare breasted in front of Mama Ajoache. The old woman removed the stones with a piece of burning firewood and placed them in a small basket. She wiped off the ash with old pieces of cloth.

Mama Ajoache spread out a mat and told me to lie on it with my back against the floor. She used the cloth to pick up the stones and as she brought them towards my breasts, my mother held down my arms so that I couldn't move.

"Abi, take heart, it won't hurt so much. She's not going to press them too hard, just a few touches and before you know it, we're through."

I was sweating profusely already. *No!* This woman would *not iron my breasts with those stones*. Hot stones on human breasts. I could not fathom such an act of savagery simply labeled "tradition". The rite is not right, I thought and as the stones came closer, several things happened in a flash.

I screamed, startling both women such that my mother's grip loosened. I raised my arms vigorously, freeing myself and slapping Mama Ajoache's hand. The stones collided and fell from her fingers onto her left toe and she winced in pain.

I sprang like a grasshopper and took off, knocking into Mama Ajoache. I heard my mother shout my name but I didn't look back. I just kept flying away like an eagle, my wrapper flapping in the wind, like wings. I held it in place with both hands. I didn't care if anything happened to me, whether I'd be cursed for not having my breasts flattened.

I reached a big boulder and sat down near the stream to rest and wash my sweating face. I was panting like a dog and dipped my hands into the water. I cupped some with my palms and splashed it on my face. It felt cold as it trickled down my body. I wiped my face thrice. Putting aside the folds of my wrapper, I pulled my underwear partly to the side and looked at the pad I had placed carefully under my vagina. It was wine red - my menses flowing again. I would have to get another pad from mother once I got home.

My heart sank when I thought about mother. What was she going to do to me? Hmmm, she would surely skin me alive. I was probably the first girl in our village to violate the ironing of breasts.

I don't know how Jimmy found me at the stream - I saw

95

him running towards me about forty-five minutes later. He was panting and looked frightened.

"What?" I asked. "How did you find me?"

"That's irrelevant Abi. The whole village knows what happened between you and Mama Ajoache. But there is a *bigger* problem."

"What problem?" I asked.

"When you bumped into Mama Ajoache, she fell and hit her head on one of the stones and fainted. She's been rushed to a hospital. It's serious."

I felt my knees go weak. We were silent, understanding the gravity of the situation.

"I, I, was just defending myself. I didn't mean it. My breasts are not meant to be ironed and deformed by hot rocks as if they are rumpled clothes to be ironed by a hot electric iron."

We both laughed but stopped quickly.

"Your actions have caused an uproar," he said. "The elderly women may be planning something against you."

"I will go to my aunt's place in Azi. It's not very far."

"Okay," he said, but I saw sadness in his eyes.

"I will come back for you my love, don't worry about me."

'Okay." He smiled. "Go and wait for me at our Kola-nut tree. I'll get you my sister's skirt and blouse so you can dress up. I don't want you walking all over the place in a loin cloth."

"And some pads!" I said.

His eyes widened. "Have you had your first menses?"

"Yes." I snapped.

"How was the experience?" he asked.

"That's woman business, Romeo!" I reproached him playfully and he laughed. I wrapped my arms around him, kissed him fully on his lips and retreated.

"Whoa, you've learnt that fast, Juliet!" he observed gripping my waist tighter.

"It tastes like orange juice," I said and he laughed again.

He caught me in a sweet embrace, "Abi, you should leave now. I'll see you at our tree okay?"

I nodded and withdrew from him. I caressed his cheeks,

turned around and started walking towards the Kola-nut tree.

THE GIFT
Michelle Preen

I sit on an upturned plastic milk crate and wait, just like I used to do every evening before this. But now I have nothing to wait for, so I count the chickens in Mrs Xingashe's backyard. Seven. The skinny one with the nearly-bald head seems to have disappeared. Maybe it died or maybe she ate it.

I look down at the watch on my wrist. It is five minutes to six. If this was two weeks ago, I would have seen my father walking down the dusty road towards me, but not today. Not ever again. I try not to cry when I think about it, but I am so angry and so sad, all mixed together, that it's hard not to. But I have to stay strong for my mother and my little sister.

I see Mr Rhadebe coming towards me, so I sniff hard and sit up straighter.

"*Molo*," says Mr Rhadebe.

"*Molo Tata*," I say.

"How is your ma, my boy?"

I am counting the feathers in his hat and he has to repeat the question.

"She is okay, thank you, *Tata*."

"Nice watch," he says.

I smile. "Thank you, my father gave it to me a few days before… before he left us."

I rub the glass with my thumb and he pats my shoulder and walks on.

"*Hamba kakuhle*," he says.

I look at my watch again. I like knowing what the time is. It makes me feel in control of my life. Lately, it feels like things have been falling apart and moving faster than I can keep up with, and this watch makes me feel better. It tells me that no matter what happens, time will remain the same. Well, not that it won't change, but it will keep on ticking along at exactly the same pace every day.

"Whatya doing?" My sister, Babalwa, bounces up to me and kicks the crate.

"Hey," I say. "Just looking at my watch."

"Let me see," she says, stretching out her hand.

"Just be careful," I say, undoing the strap and handing it to her.

"I will, silly." She holds it in her hand then turns it over. "What's this say?" she asks.

I hadn't paid much attention to the writing engraved on the back before. I knew my father had bought it second-hand. He could not have afforded a new watch for me. But now it somehow seems more important, so I read it out to her.

"It says *the gift of time*".

"What does that mean?" she asks. She crinkles up her nose and tilts her head on one side, waiting for my answer.

"I suppose it means that someone gave the watch to someone else as a present."

My father died twelve days ago. He worked in the kitchen at a fish and chips restaurant in the nearby shopping mall. I was seven years old when he started that job, so he must have been working there for about five years. Everyone who ate there liked him, or that is what the story in the local newspaper said anyway. I never met any of them.

He sometimes used to bring home a piece of fish for us. Once he told us he even tried a prawn. I am not sure if I would have been that brave. Prawns are strange creatures, like pink sea insects, and I have heard that they eat the rubbish off the ocean floor.

"I grew up eating red meat," my father used to say, embarrassed that he was bringing us fish. Red meat is expensive, so to make him feel better I told him that our teacher had said that too much red meat could be bad for your heart, but he wouldn't hear of it. "It's good for you, my boy," he always said. I loved my father.

Twelve nights ago, it was a Saturday night. He was working night shift at the restaurant instead of during the day as he usually did. My mother had allowed my sister and me to stay up and wait for him because it wasn't a school night, but he never arrived home when he was meant to.

At about 11:35 – I knew this because I checked my watch – we heard shouting in the street and my mother peeped out of the door of our shack to see what was happening. It isn't safe to just step outside in the middle of the night, especially if there is a commotion. I heard her cry out and I ran out behind her, pushing her aside. I saw my father covered in blood and being helped along by a neighbour. His head was hanging, just lolling around as if he had no control over his neck. His blue and white checked shirt was torn and soaked in blood and some of it had even spattered onto his beige pants. He loved those pants and took such great care of them, and all I could think about was that he was going to be upset when he saw that they had been stained by the blood, his blood.

I can't remember much about what happened next because my mother was crying so much, and I was trying to stay strong and comfort her and Babs. That's what I call my sister. The neighbour called an ambulance on his cell phone and we waited and waited. I wasn't allowed to talk to my father because my mother said he needed his energy to stay alive. So I just sat there, with my arm around Babs, and I prayed that my father would live and that we would be able to get the blood stains out of his pants.

The ambulance took a long time to arrive so I counted the second hand on my watch while we waited. It could have been an hour, but it may have been more. They put my father on a stretcher and took him away and that was the last time I ever saw him. They didn't put the sirens on and I remember wondering if that was a good thing or a bad thing. It seemed to suggest that they weren't in a hurry.

The newspaper said he was a hero and so did my teacher. They said that he had tried to protect a young girl who was being attacked by a bad man with a knife, that my father had come between them and been stabbed by the man. They said he had saved the girl. I felt proud of him, but also cross with him because he had risked his life for a girl we didn't even know, and now what about us, his own family. This is wrong of me, I know, but I can't help feeling like that. I miss my father.

The newspaper people asked my mother and me if we would like to meet the girl so that they could take a photograph, but I said no. All I would see in her eyes would be my father's face. My mother was much more understanding. She agreed to meet the girl, who wanted to thank her, but she refused to have a photograph taken. My mother is superstitious about photographs and believes that they steal away a little bit of your soul.

People in our community talk and some of them know lots of things. By now, we all know who killed my father. But he probably won't be arrested. And even if he is, I am not sure if he will be properly punished. People are scared to be witnesses and so he would more than likely just spend a night in jail and then be let out again to attack another young girl and steal someone else's father from them. I pray that it will not be my sister that is attacked.

He's called *Ithoba*, the man who killed my father. That means *nine*. He's mean-looking and doesn't talk much, they say. I don't know if he was given that name because he has nine lives like a cat or if he has taken nine lives, like a murderer. Maybe it's both.

I kick the gravel with the toe of my shoe. I own two pairs – *this* pair are black leather lace-ups that I use for school, and a pair of rubber flip-flops. My flip-flops are blue. I would rather have had red ones but a lady who felt sorry for me gave them to me after she heard my father was killed, so I couldn't choose the colour.

We were also given food and some blankets by a charity when my father died. They usually give people blankets when there is a flood or a fire, and you lose all your things. I guess maybe they had some blankets left over or didn't know what else to give us. My mother is always grateful for anything though, and now that winter is coming the blankets will be useful. There was a pink and purple checked one, which my sister liked. She asked if she could have it and now she takes it everywhere with her, even to school. My mother is worried about that but I said that I think she just needs comfort after losing my father.

"Hey," says Babs, "who did the watch belong to before you got it?"

I had forgotten she was standing there. Her hair is tied in three neat bunches, one on each side and one in the middle, and she is holding her blanket, which doesn't look as bright as it did ten days ago.

"Dunno," I say.The busy sounds of a weekday evening fill the smoky air

around us. Dogs bark, taxis rev their engines and people talk and shout to one another as they come home after a day at work or school. Many people crowd around open fires trying to warm their chilled hands. It feels like I am on the outside looking in on their world.

I struggle to sleep that night. For some reason, my sister's question keeps running around in my mind, going round and round in circles. I begin to feel that maybe I need to find out who the watch belonged to before me. It will also be a way to find out what my father was doing those last few days before he died. I know he sometimes bought presents for us from the animal shelter's second-hand shop quite close to my school. So, after school the next day, I decide to go there and ask.

The old lady in the shop looks at me suspiciously when I ask if a handsome black man bought a watch there about two weeks ago.

"Why do you want to know, sonny?" she asks.

"Because it's important to me," I say.

"I can't go about telling you other people's business, now can I?" she says. She walks off with a feather duster in her hand to dust the bookshelves, but I follow her.

"Excuse me," I say, "this is the watch." I hold out my wrist to her. "Can you at least tell me if you sold it?"

She turns around slowly and peers at me. It looks as if she can't see that well, so I hold it up closer to her face. As she's about to answer, a young woman runs in through the door.

"Sorry I'm late," she calls. "Still struggling to get up in the mornings." She looks sad and her hair is messy.

She comes over to us and says: "So what do we have here?"

"He's asking about the watch," says the old lady.

"Let me see," says the young one with messy hair.

"Aha." "What?" I say. "Do you recognise it?"

"Uhu," she says.

I look from one to the other, hoping for more information.

"Why don't you come through to the back with me," the young one says, "and we'll have a nice cup of tea? You don't mind, do you Mrs Maytham?" She doesn't wait for an answer and takes my hand.

I sit on an old wooden chair while she makes a cup of tea for each of us.

"Two sugars?" she asks, but before I can answer she pops them in and hands me a mug. She wraps her long skirt around her knees and sits cross-legged on the floor in front of me.

"Yes, that watch," she says.

"Would you like to sit on the chair?" I ask. There is only one.

"Nope."

I can see her ankle peeping out from under her skirt. There are three flying swallows tattooed on it.

"So, who owned this watch?" I ask.

"Me," she says. "Well, not really me. I gave it to my husband."

"Why did he sell it, then?" I am starting to worry that maybe someone stole it and now she might want it back. I rub the glass with my thumb.

"He didn't," she says. "I did."

"Oh," I say, "why?" I hope he didn't divorce her and now she's going to be sad and cry and I won't know what to say.

"He died," she says.

Now I definitely don't know what to say. I wasn't expecting that. She is so young.

"Don't worry," she says. "I won't cry."

She must have read my mind.

"Someone shot him," she says. "He was a policeman and he died in a shoot-out. I had given him the watch a few days before as an anniversary present. I had those words engraved on it because I thought we had so much time ahead of us, that we were still so young. We'd only been married for a year"

Then I see a tear run down her cheek.

"I'm so sorry," is all I can think of to say.

"Get rid of it," she says, "it's cursed. If you don't get rid of it something bad will happen to you or your family."

"It already has," I say. "My father was killed twelve days ago. He gave me the watch."

"Oh my goodness!" she says "It is true."

103

Mrs Maytham is now peering around the floral curtain which separates the back room from the front of the shop.

"I need a break," she says to the young woman, whose name I still don't know.

She gulps down the last mouthfuls of her tea and jumps up.

"Get rid of it," she says once more, before patting me on the shoulder and disappearing through the curtain and into the shop.

"You can go out the back door," says Mrs Maytham to me.

I think about it all the way home. I love this watch. It's the last thing my father gave me. It's one of my only links to him. But what if it is cursed? What if something bad happens to my mother or sister? Crime is so bad in South Africa though. People get shot all the time, so maybe it's just a co-incidence. He was a policeman. But what about my father? He just tried to save someone. I love my watch. I loved my father. I love my father.

Just before I go to sleep that night, I say aloud: "What should I do, father? Please help me." I am not sure if he can hear me, but I hope he will put an idea into my mind. When I wake up the next morning, the radio is on. It's playing a song which goes 'there are nine million bicycles in Beijing'.

"Nine," my sister shouts, "nine million? Is that true? Where is Beijing?"

As my mother puts down my porridge on the table in front of me, I know what I must do. My father has spoken to me through the radio. I cannot concentrate at school. I am nervous, but excited at the same time.

At midnight when I am sure most people are asleep, I throw off my blankets and sneak out of our shack. The door hinges squeak but neither my mother nor my sister move. I stand still for a few seconds just to make sure. Then I start to run, down our road, then left past six shacks, then right, then right again, down the next road, past the Spaza shop and the shebeen, then here I am. I planned this all in the afternoon during daylight so I would know exactly where to go. It looks different at night, but I have a good memory.

I stand in front of a shack. It looks like all the others, but this one has the number '9' painted in black on the door. But this isn't just any old nine. The round part of the nine is a skull. I am breathing fast and I can feel my heart in my chest. I place my right hand over my watch. Then I undo the buckle. I hold it in my left hand so that my right hand is free to open the door. I am sweating. They told me the door would be open because he is afraid of nothing. I am frightened. I walk towards the door, being careful to step quietly. I can hear someone snoring inside. At least he is asleep. I reach out to the handle and turn it slowly, then push the door a little way. It doesn't creak and he is still snoring. I push it further then just stand there and look at him. I want to scream or hit him, sleeping so peacefully while my father is dead. But I know that would get me nowhere. It would probably get me killed too. I have another weapon. I tiptoe over to the small round table next to his bed and place the watch on it next to the empty quart of Black Label beer. I smile, no longer afraid.

"May you be cursed with *the gift of time*," I whisper, and creep out into the dark night.

THE WOUND OF SHRINKING
Melissa Kiguwa

I wouldn't be surprised if my mother committed suicide. She's insinuated doing it since I was twelve years old. She'd say, *Oh Solo...you know I'm not good at anything. I'm not even a good mother. If I died, it'd be a blessing I think.*

At thirteen I tried to birth her desert roses, those impossible kinds that even bloom on land- locked islands. But she couldn't see the roses springing from the openings in my body. The roots coming from my eyes the stems from my nose. At fourteen, sinewy fibres vined their way down and porous mucous sapped from the inside of my ears. But she couldn't see any of it.

Perhaps that is where my *woundedness* was born, from constantly trying to push something from my womb that wasn't mine to carry. I would think, there must be something I can do - should do - to make the noise around us less shrill.

I felt maybe if I were better behaved and quieter, maybe then she would realize her place was with me. I tried to be quiet. I'd pull my lips in real tight so that I couldn't say a word ... But ten minutes in and my motor mouth would rev its engine.

At eighteen I felt like a weary dark-skinned Atlas. So I let it go, dropped the wound on its head and watched it roll away. I decided to focus on her brighter parts instead, those disorienting dissonances housed in one body. How she could weave the spiritual into the theoretical. How she lived in a room of moving colours and how the muses housed in her brain would craft beauty from the mundane. I always secretly wished she would give in to the artisan that sat inside her fingers. But she would get discouraged and pieces of majik would sit a dusty kind of lonely in the back of her room.

The first year of Moses's and my relationship, whenever I spent the night I would ask him to tell me when to leave so that I didn't bother him. He would sigh and ask why he would be in a relationship with someone whose presence bothered him. But how could he know I had started carrying it again? The wound of shrinking. And even though I told myself to believe him when he said he wanted me around, I still felt that tapping sound. The knock that whispered, you have overstayed your welcome, it's time to go.

So I would watch him. The curvature of his mouth. The patterns of his footsteps. Any ritual that signified he was ready to be left to his solitude. And if you are looking, you will always find. I would find it, there inside the curvature when I said something he disagreed with. His lips would turn downward as though I had squeezed pili-pili on the insides of his mouth. And when I saw it I knew it was time to leave before I broke something I didn't know the shape of.

But somehow he convinced me that perhaps, yes, with him is where I should be. I mean he even knew about the years I fell in love with a radical politic and other women. He eroticized it I think...the musky smells that at one time were my North Stars signaling me to realizations away from this one. But even though he knew of sexual acts, I knew he couldn't understand that I had been desperately searching for life in the crevices of those women's bodies. And today *that* Solome, the desperately searching one, is far away for him. But that Solome understands today's one. The one who no longer searches for life, but for purpose everywhere ... And can't find it anywhere.

At twenty-five, I realize purpose has left me. Stretched along Moses's bed, I prop myself up with a sigh and dial my mother's number. I want to talk about the tunnel that seems to stretch into nothingness...how it could be hell, a purgatory limbo, or even heaven itself. The stoic nothingness that chills its way into my body until even my heart doesn't want to pump anymore. Instead, I tell her about Ngenyo.

I think the name Ngenyo does not make sense for me at this point in my life, I say into the mouthpiece. *I don't know what it means or where it comes from! And I get so embarrassed when people ask, where is your name from? What does your name mean? And I have no answers. I can't be this old still dealing with identity shame!*

Ngenyo, Ngenyo ... We've real tried and tried to get a name or a number ... Anything to give you some kind of an anchor, she says.

I know, I croon. *I wish jaajaa gave us something! This*

whole thing has been so tiring ... Stalkers masquerading as cousins ... Clan meetings held without me to resume some long-standing ritual ... Realising jaajaa disowned everybody, except me, with the last name Ngenyo! I didn't realize how stubborn he was until he consistently refused to give us any information.

Moses's phone rings and my mother, laughing, asks, *mafia girl, how many phones do you have?*

I pick up the phone facing downwards on the table next to the bed and see the letter T. I silence the ringer quickly. *Sorry about that ... Anyway, mom, even Joseph ...*

You mean your father?

Yes, him.

She sighs. *You've always been a writer Solo. I remember all the stories you wrote when you were a teenager ... Even after you went to university. There would always be one character ... Let me see if I remember the wording correctly ... You wrote about a quiet man with glasses that reminded you of pictures of Patrice Lumumba. No matter how many times you wrote it, it always caught me unaware.*

What caught you? I ask, a bit irritated that she cut me off.

The way you could do that ... Capture the essence of a man in a sentence.

I smile, flattered. *Well memories split. There is him, with the glasses, and then there are other patchy memories, the ones after the separation. Was it really him, flighty and hostile, banging on our door in London with police officers behind him?*

Yes, she replies slowly, each letter suspended between the receivers next to our mouths.

I visited with Joseph about five times after they separated, each time in a new residence. Once in someone's garage, another time in a friend's guest room, the other three locations silhouettes I can never place. The pictures of my mother during this time show a shell. Her cheeks sunken, her legs the size of twigs. She laughs when she sees I carry them in my wallet. *You surely are a weird child, Solo. Why would you want to keep pictures of such an ugly woman? Look, you can even see the bones under my eyes!*

I don't know when we stopped referring to Joseph Ngenyo outside of family reunions. We learnt not to grieve over people who leave. I learnt, first from my mother, to fill the memory of emptiness through one-way tickets to places further away from the cradle of betrayal.

When she speaks again, her voice sounds like a faraway lighthouse beckoning me back, *will you change your names into something more traditional and African-y?* She asks. I laugh.

No seriously Solo, she says quickly, *I know it's what's hip with the Pan-Africanists … I'm just waiting to read a poem by Olumide Ngenyo formerly known as Solome.*

I laugh again, *this time from somewhere deep and ringing. Olumide is so far from my reality! If you ever read a poem by Olumide Ngenyo formerly known as Solome, please give me a nice big mstcheeew slap over the phone!*

She giggles. *You haven't answered my question. Are you going to keep Solome?*

I mean … I've definitely thought about changing it. Especially when I first began going to these Afro events. Man, the way they Malcolm X us all into believing anything that seems relatively mainstream, read white, is somehow a false consciousness. But I think some things are a bit deeper than that. When you named me Solome, you did so with intention.

And what intention was that?

Well … The skin of sound is sometimes thick and taut, veiny and melanin rich. And I have fallen into the sound … Or rather the skin.

My God, she interrupts, *where did you learn to become so melodramatic?*

I ignore the question and continue. *From me, Solome, to you, Sarah, whose mother named you a Biblical skin, to your mother, Juliet, who was grafted a skin of Latin derivatives. Three generations laden in a grip so tightly wound only we can see a reflection of something other than oppressed. I see it: the whiteness, the syllables that pray difficult on relatives' lips...but still how can I change my name? As though I am ashamed of your decisions …*

She interrupts me again, *but it was Malcolm X who said he does not know his name because it was a slave name, hence the X. That his father did not know his name either and his father's father because they were given names of the white man. There's that story too Solo, the story of erasure.*

I tell her, *my story lies in you naming me. While it may not speak to nativity the way some would like to romanticise it, it does speak to our reality of passage, of conversion, and yes, of too much luzungu in our mouths.*

She is quiet and I wonder if the international package on the phone I bought has finished. *You know I was just reading about a tribe, I do not remember which but they have a practice that is so interesting ...* She pauses and sucks in air before she continues, *well before a mother gives birth she goes to a tree. I'm not sure how the tree is picked, but it is picked and she goes to the tree and listens. Inside the tree plays her child's song and as she listens she memorises it. When the baby is born, she sings the song. And that is how it is ... Anytime the child covers a milestone or a rite of passage, the child's song is sung ... I read that and thought, my goodness! Maybe if I had a song life wouldn't have turned out this way for me you know? If only... well, anyway, even when the child messes up, you know maybe becomes a thief or something, the family gathers and calls the child. They sing the song and it is up to the child to choose whether she or he wants to return to goodness ...*

She finishes her story and I sigh again, *that is so beautiful.*

Yeah, I thought so too. I remembered it when you told me the reason you wanted to keep the name Solome.

I smile into the phone. I want to sing her a song or offer her a gift of re-birthed desert-roses, but we never say the words that are most honest.

She interrupts my thoughts. *Well ... It is getting quite late your side and I know your credit is about to finish, love you.*

Love you too.

We get off the phone and I climb off the bed and stretch a bit. I decide to check on Moses and walk downstairs.

He is asleep on the couch; I watch him sprawled like an unending question and try to figure out where I can squeeze myself in. I slide next to him, now the both of us curled into a pair.

Skin to skin the only thing clearly distinct between us, heartbeat and even the rhythm harmonises after some time.

With his mouth open the way it is, I imagine a dark-hollowed tunnel where steam-engines get lost. Destination: beyond the limitation of boundaries and borders. But even I know it is never that simple. He shifts and sighs while snuggling me closer. *Babe, I can hear you thinking.*

I fall asleep snuggled next to him but his phone rings upstairs and I wake up with a start. I look at the lighted clock on the desk and ask, *it's past midnight and your phone is ringing?*

Probably a silly telecom or something, he mumbles half asleep slowly nudging me off the sofa so we can go to bed.

The next day, I have lunch with a colleague. *Moses is really a catch,* she says as though I asked her opinion. *Handsome, educated, successful. I mean ... Every educated Ugandan woman is trying to meet such a guy ... Perhaps if we all had that American accent of yours we would have a chance.*

You really believe the only reason Moses is attracted to me is because of my accent?

She looks at me incredulously. *Honestly the only reason you were able to meet him is because of your diaspora privilege!*

I never know what weight to give such comments because to her, all things I do and say are viewed within the lens of diaspora privilege. But the nuances within desire and power are too mired for me to examine during lunch on a Friday, so I joke instead: *Honey, with this face and booty, regardless of which country I'm in, I never have a problem getting successful, handsome dates!*

She smiles at the joke in a fake kind of way.

Moses makes his pili-pili face when I tell him about the conversation. We are home from work lying on the sofa. He is seated upright and my head is on his lap, my torso foetal-position curved and my legs stretched across the rest of the couch. Miles Davis is playing and he slowly uses his index finger to tap elongated time signatures on my forehead.

He looks at me and stops tapping, *privilege is a heavy word. I think these things have more depth than whatever she is jealous about. I think the real underlying point to take away is that you need to have lunch with other people.*

I remind him it's not just this person. That we are

immersed in a global culture that values some bodies more than others. *Valued bodies, if not white, tend to speak a certain kind of English. They tend to be groomed bourgeoisie in a certain way, and when you can play the game, the playing field is completely different. It's important to know the ways in which cultural power structures position one's body and experiences as valuable because it does so at the expense of others.*

Oh my god, he says rolling his eyes. *Edward Said called, he wants his thesis back.*

I smile and roll my eyes back at him. As he smiles at me, I search to find it in his face. The rescue boat that will pull me away from an inherited depression and closer to a grounded shore.

Later that night, I revel in his tight grip. In the middle of making love, his phone rings. Because I'm on top, I see the flashing phone on the drawer. The letter T flashes and I'm suddenly un-aroused.

Moses looks at me with a face I don't recognize. *Why the hell would someone call me three o' clock in the morning?*

I look him in the eye, *I don't know …. It's probably important. Pick it up.*

Nah, they can call tomorrow. By this time I'm climbing off of him. *Baby, come back,* he pleads. *Where you going?* I walk to the toilet and bang the door shut.

Babe, I hear his voice a few minutes later. *You've been in there for a while. I miss you … You left me hanging. Come back to bed.*

I shake my head, *I'll be in here for a while.*

I hear his footsteps moving back to the bedroom. I somehow muster the strength to walk out of the bathroom and crawl back into bed. With my back turned to him, I curl into myself. Wrapping himself around me, he begins kissing the nape of my neck. *Not right now,* I say into the pillow, my voice drowned but still audible.

That's alright, baby, that's alright. Let's get some rest then, he purrs in my ear.

My mother calls me in the morning to check in. Our conversation is brief because it is one in the morning her time.

Right before she says bye I ask, *Mom let me ask you, what*

is better
to use, the head or the heart?

She pauses, *Solome ... I'm surprised you have to ask. Remember when we were in the storm ... The belly of the beast I guess you could call it? We went through those tough times together and you know better than I do that the head is what led us to better places. If I followed my heart, we would not be where we are. We would just be ... Confused, I guess. It is always the head, Solo, always the head.*

I want to joke that we are still confused, that she was right all along ... We could end chasing all of this vanity by not waking up the next morning, but it seems today I have learnt to pull in my lips.

I have dinner with a close friend later in the evening. *But Otieno, why are you single again?* I ask mischievously. *It just doesn't make sense!*

He smiles. *You know I am married to my work.*

I understand that it is easier to be accountable to something that does not demand an emotional investment, but to be thirty and accountable to nothing? What are you running from?

He looks at me. *I should be asking you the same question, Solo.*

How do I say that I searched everywhere for the wound to stop throbbing, but that it refused? How do I say I am running from the cradle of betrayal?

About the Authors

Wise Ngasa Nzikie (Cameroon)

Wise Ngasa Nzikie's father introduced him to novels as a child. He would read a novel and think about the words in them for days. Words make noises in his head. They talk to him, so he writes them. As an activist and social entrepreneur, he writes against exploitation. He writes to provoke, to annoy, to insult, to change. He is 28 years old and holds a BSc. in Accountancy. He is currently undertaking a Masters in International Development at the Institute of Education of the University of London. He is the Founder of Action Foundation, a leading youth-development CSO in Africa. His Writivism Short Story Prize shortlisted story is Devils.

Saaleha Bhamjee (South Africa)

Saaleha Bhamjee writes between mothering five children and running her bakery. A self-confessed Twitterholic, she blogs at http://afrocentric-muslimah.blogspot.com/. She was part of the Cape Town February Writivism workshops and the online mentoring program. Her shortlisted story is titled Lunatic.

Saaleha Idrees Bamjee (South Africa)

Saaleha Idrees Bamjee is a freelance writer, photographer and incidental designer who lives and works in Johannesburg, South Africa. She has an MA in Creative Writing from Rhodes University, Grahamstown. Her poetry has appeared in South African literary journals and can also be read online at www.saaleha.com. She is one of the 2014 Writivism workshop participants in Cape Town, and was also a mentee under the Writivism mentoring program. Her shortlisted story is titled Out of the Blue.

Kelechi Njoku (Nigeria)

Kelechi Njoku is a broadcast journalist. His short stories and non-fiction have been published in the Kalahari Review, Nigerians Talk LitMag, Reindeer, Aerodrome, My Mind Snaps, Africa Book Club, The Clip and the Naija Stories anthology Reflections of

Sunshine. He lives in Abuja. His Writivism Short Story Prize shortlisted story is titled Survived By.

Ssekandi Ssegujja Ronald (Uganda)

Ssekandi Ssegujja Ronald is a writer, poet and law student. He is also the Executive Director of Writing Our World, a youth-run NGO in Uganda working with and empowering young writers to contribute to positive change in their communities. He has a keen interest in spoken word and the power of the arts in changing our world. He is also a Peace Fellow of The DO School in Germany and a member of the Ugandan Youth Advisors to Washington. His shortlisted story is titled Walls and Borders.

Arnold Ngoda Musalia (Kenya)

Arnold Ngoda Musalia was born in 1988, in Nairobi, Kenya. He holds a diploma certificate in Electronic Media from Daystar University (2011). He has just finished pursuing his degree in Communications (Public Relations) at the same institution and expects to graduate on June 28th 2014. 'Kawesa', his Writivism Short Story Prize longlisted story, is his first story.

Chumisa Paquita N (South Africa)

Chumisa Paquita N is a 24 year old scriptwriter based in Cape Town. She writes and reads about black consciousness, daydreams and fantastical things. Apart from work and attending live music performances, her life is about finding her way to Assata Shakur. She was part of the Cape Town Writivism workshop and mentoring program. Her longlisted story is Friday Night.

Nyachiro Lydia Kasese (Tanzania)

Nyachiro Lydia Kasese is a twenty-two-year-old Tanzanian. Having been raised in four other African countries she is multilingual. She studied Industrial and Economic Sociology at the University of Rhodes. She currently works as a writer and journalist, among other things, in Dar-es-salaam, Tanzania. Nyachiro was part of the 2014 Writivism Mentoring program and her longlisted story is Inside Outside.

Melissa Kiguwa (Uganda)

Melissa Kiguwa is an artist, a daughter, and a radical feminist. Her work is rooted in acknowledging and giving praise to diverse global afro-experiences. Her work focuses on imperialism, migration, sexuality, spirituality, and trauma. In her work she re-imagines liberation, new horizons, and inter-generational legacy building. Kiguwa was a participant in the 2014 Writivism Workshop in Kampala, and took part in the mentoring program. Her Writivism longlisted story is The Wound of Shrinking.

Michelle Preen (South Africa)

Michelle Preen lives in Cape Town. She is a graduate from the University of Kwazulu-Natal and currently works in the field of environmental communications and media. She has had short stories published in various anthologies and magazines. You can follow Michelle on Twitter @mpreen or www.michellepreen.com. She was one of the participants at the Cape Town Writivism workshop in February 2014 and has been a mentee on the program. Her longlisted story is The Gift.

Myke Mwale (Zimbabwe)

Myke Mwale is a Zimbabwean, currently studying in South Africa. In 2010 his play Mandida's Shoes was shortlisted and broadcasted for the BBC African Performance. He is interested in exploring the 'other story'. His longlisted story, Fire in the Night, exposes this interest. Mike has recently completed his studies in Ethics.

Nkiacha Atemnkeng (Cameroon)

Nkiacha Atemnkeng is a Cameroonian writer, book reviewer and blogger at nkiachaatemnkeng.blogspot.com. He was shortlisted for the 2013 Mardibooks Short Story competition. A holder of a Curriculum Studies/Biology degree from the University of Buea in Cameroon, he works as a Swissport Customer Service agent at the Douala International Airport. Nkiacha's longlisted story is titled My Breasts.

Paul Ugbede (Nigeria)

Paul Ugbede was a part of the Writivism 2014 short story workshop in Abuja Nigeria, facilitated by Ukamaka Olisakwe and Abubakar Adam Ibrahim. He also participated in the Chimamanda/Fidelity Bank Creative Writing Workshop. He resides in Lagos, Nigeria, where he is the Managing Editor of Golfers Africa Magazine. His longlisted story is titled Day after Tomorrow.

Wale Lawal (Nigeria)

Wale Lawal has a B.Sc. in Economics from the University of Bath. Presently, he resides in Lagos and teaches at a government school. Via his Twitter page, @WalleLawal, he documents a personal literary project centred on Lagos women. In October, he will be joining the London School of Economics for postgraduate studies in History. His Writivism short story prize longlisted story is Dr. Lawanson.

Acknowledgements

This year the Writivism program widened its reach to embrace the entire continent, abolishing the ageist limitations on the definition of emerging writers. The resultant growth in scope and impact is evident in the numbers of emerging and established writers that have been engaged in this year's cycle.

At the apex we have worked with six prominent personalities in the African literature sector, namely Zukiswa Wanner, Lizzy Attree, EC Osondu, NoViolet Bulawayo, Chika Unigwe and Ayikwei Nii Parkes, as members of our Board of Trustees. Our panel of judges for the short story prize included Ellen Banda-Aaku as Chair, Zukiswa Wanner (chair of the 2013 prize), Emmanuel Sigauke, Abubakar Adam Ibrahim and Glaydah Namukasa.

We held five workshops in five different African cities: Abuja, Harare, Kampala, Nairobi and Cape Town. They were facilitated by Zukiswa Wanner, Ukamaka Olisakwe, Rachel Zadok, Memory Chirere, Monica Cheru, Abubakar Adam Ibrahim and Glaydah Namukasa. More than 60 emerging writers were recruited into our mentoring program at the workshops. We had twenty mentors, each of whom mentored one to five emerging writers. The mentors were Okwiri Oduor, Ukamaka Olisakwe, Rachel Zadok, Monica Cheru, Yewande Omotoso, Samuel Kolawole, Dilman Dila, Julius Sseremba, Sumayya Lee, Barbara Mhangami-Ruwende, Juliane Okot Bitek, Kiprop Timothy Kimutai, Michael Onsando, Lauri Kubuitsile, Dr. Sylva Nze Ifedigbo, Richard Ali, Dami Ajayi, Tendai Mwanaka, Gothataone Moeng and Clifton Gachagua.

In total the program has engaged over 100 African writers, both established and emerging. The growth in the impact of the program is most visible in the increase in the entries for the short story prize. There were over 200 entries for the short story prize this year, compared to 50 in the previous year. The growth is also noticeable in the improvement in the quality of longlisted stories. We also have expanded the scope of the mentoring, beyond flash fiction, to include short fiction writing. Thus, whereas in our first year we only dealt with flash fiction, this year writers on the mentoring program produced both flash and short fiction. The flash fiction was published all over the continent. We were also pleased to welcome our new media partners Books Live of South Africa, Sunday Trust of Nigeria, Deyu African and Muwado; and of course we remain grateful to our initial media partner, The Observer, for always being there for us.

We kept with Short Story Day Africa and, in fact, deepened our relationship with the initiative to the point of a near-merger. We got excited with them when Okwiri Oduor and Efemie Chela, both engaged with Writivism as mentor and workshop participant respectively, and whose two stories were published in the Short Story Day Africa anthology Famine, Feast and Potluck, were each shortlisted for the Caine Prize for African Writing. Munyori Literary Journal too kept supporting us.

On the financial support front, the Open Society Initiative for Eastern Africa has remained faithful to us, and we added the Danish Centre for Culture and Development to the fold of our supporters. The Prince Claus Fund Ticket Grants have helped us to host writers from other countries at the annual Writivism Festival. That is another proof of our growth. From a three-day event, held at a university guest house in 2013, we are now swimming with the big fish at Uganda's premier arts venue, the National Theatre, thanks to a partnership with the Uganda National Cultural Centre. The Writivism Festival now lasts five full days.

I have tried to thank everyone for the work they have done on the entire Writivism program, but I have not yet thanked everyone of course. Those unmentioned above, your input is valued too. This anthology would not have been possible without the hard work of two people, Ceris Dien of Kushinda who complied and formatted the publishing files, and Sumayya Lee, our editor for this year. In a short time, after the announcement of the longlist, these two worked with the longlisted writers and the prize judges to sweeten the meal that this anthology is. We are indebted to them for the work to which we can't attach a price.

All our staff at CACE, paid and unpaid, without your love and effort nothing could come out of our dreaming. We are grateful and hope you continue to offer your awesomeness to what we believe is a great cause.

For the reader, Writivism is as much about the writer as it is about you. Thanks for reading the flash fiction published in the various media on the continent. Thanks for reading the five shortlisted stories on our Writivism blog, Munyori Literary Journal and Short Story Day Africa. We are excited to present to you all the fourteen longlisted stories for your enjoyment.

See you next year when we release yet another Writivism Anthology.

Bwesigye bwa Mwesigire